TRIBE of BLONDES™

Adventures Of
Break Up Survivors
Seeking Love Online
& Happiness
In Relationships

HADLEY FINCH

Author's
PUBLISHER
The New Generation of Publishing

TRIBE of BLONDES™

Adventures of Break Up Survivors Seeking Love Online & Happiness In Relationships

A Novel by Hadley Finch

ISBN: 978-0-9817009-4-6 Paperback

Published by:

Author's Publisher
14805 Forest Road, Suite 106
Forest, VA 24551
www.AuthorsPublisher.com

Cover & Interior Design by:
Heather Kirk
www.BrandedForSuccess.com

Cover Concept & Art by:
Pearl Planet Design
www.pearl-planet.net

The Birth of the TRIBE of BLONDES

Hadley Finch's debut novel and bonus album of songs are inspired by her real-life journey from lost love to the Fire Of Love. When her valiant efforts to save her two-decade marriage fail, Hadley survives her break up, revives her dreams and starts a quest for the next great love of her life.

Hadley doesn't make these great strides alone, though. She has the support of savvy men and women friends, whom she affectionately calls the *Tribe Of Blondes*.

Not a hair color, it's a resilient, hopeful spirit that gives the *Tribe* its name. We're all born with this spirit. The secret is to keep it alive. In this spirit, Hadley transforms a painful breakup into a rebirth and enchanting adventure of starting fresh and loving again—with a little help from the *Tribe of Blondes*.

Lost love is a muse I'd love to refuse
Till pain helps me see unseeable truths
I'm part of all I love, part of all I see
Can't break the thread of *Love's Tapestry*

1. MOUNTAINS vs. MEN

I started writing songs to survive the pain when my husband, Walter, left me after twenty-five years of marriage. All I could think about was what I lost—so while Walter dated Tina, a girl half his age, I wrote lyrics filled with jealousy and rage.

During the first year of our separation, the only relief I felt was on the nights Walter snuck upstairs to visit me in our bedroom, usually after each dinner he'd scheduled with our children, Logan and Jade (14 and 12 at the time he left home).

With each romantic rendezvous, Walter and I were struck by the same lightning bolt of passion we'd enjoyed throughout our first decade together. The threat of losing him to a younger lover reignited that dormant passion, and I promised Walter I wouldn't let family duties get between us again, when he came back to me for good.

"Don't get your hopes up, Hadley," he'd said. But I still believed he'd snap out of that girl's spell and come home where he belonged.

Wrapped in Walter's arms after another breathtaking reunion, something made me ask the question I'd been afraid to ask for months. "How can you go back to her when we're on fire again?"

With his fingertips, he feathered circles on my lower back, like he used to do to ease my stress, and spoke softly. "Loving sex with you doesn't mean I still love you."

I couldn't speak. Or breathe. The mechanical way he got dressed told me what was coming next, and I didn't want to hear it. "I'm sorry," he'd said, in a tone that gave me chills. "It's time to start the next chapter of our lives."

As I watched him leave me to go back to Tina, my heart rattled like a pressure cooker ready to blow. I knew I couldn't withstand the torture of loving and losing him again and again, so I had to shut down to save my life. I tried for one week, but I couldn't shut the door on the only man I've ever loved. So I enabled him to use a revolving door between his Chicago girl and his suburban wife for the next year.

In doing so, my jealousy rose to a breaking point. My mental pictures of his love scenes with her had kept me awake each night for months, while I plotted various ways to murder him and his mistress.

When I started shooting lessons at a range near my vacation home in Santa Fe, New Mexico, something inside me said, *Whoa*. Yet my violent urges were so strong I had to act on them. Fortunately, I put down my pistol and picked up a pen to find a remedy that let me **Rest In Peace**—

> **Dead, you can't hurt me anymore.**
> **This way, we have an even score.**
> **Now you let me rest in peace.**
> **Yes, I rest best. I can get some rest.**
> **Yes, I rest best when you are dead.**

Whacking Walter and Tina in a song kept them alive and me out of jail. Nevertheless, I felt anxious all the time. I lost twenty pounds. I lost a dozen china plates, when I smashed them against the floor as Walter moved his clothes out of our house.

We'd rarely argued during our marriage, so I didn't recognize the banshee I'd become during our divorce—though only when our children weren't around to see it. For their wellbeing, I stayed calm and bit my tongue instead of criticizing their dad and Tina.

Apparently, I couldn't hide the visible signs of a broken heart. When I drove our son, Logan, to his hockey game one night, he said, "We love you, Mom, even if Dad doesn't."

From the back seat our daughter, Jade said, "We'll never leave you."

I knew they loved me but I also knew they'd leave me. I wanted to say something positive, but I couldn't speak without crying. So I nodded, regretting the ways we stole their joy.

The day I read Walter's divorce papers, filed 13 months into our passionate separation, I finally gave up hope we'd reunite. I knelt at my well of grief and poured it into lyrics for **Song Unsung—**

> **My heart hurts from his betrayal**
> **I tried to right, to right his wrongs**
> **I tried to teach him a lesson**
> **That was mine all along**
> **Our marriage died with its *Song Unsung*...**

My grief couldn't be emptied into a song. Dimming my view of life's beauty, grief was a dark veil that I couldn't lift without help. My divorce lawyer told me I could call him any time I needed to talk. So I tried that. After my first call cost 400 bucks for an hour of empathy, I turned to my savvy divorced friend, Sharon Milton, for advice.

I'd met Sharon ten years earlier, when our then-husbands were inducted into Young Corporate Presidents Organization. Her husband, Roger, had left her for a baby-woman five years before Walter left me, so she had experience I lacked and often tapped into.

While lunching near divorce court where my legal wrangling had just begun, she told me the secret of how she eased the heartbreak of her high-profile divorce:

"Get a lover," she said. "You'll detach from Walter by dating ten men for each year you were married."

"Date 250 men?" I shrieked. That got people's attention at surrounding tables.

"For a healthy start," she said. "You don't know the new you yet, so you can't possibly know what you want in a new man. Know why most second marriages fail?"

"No clue."

"People dive in before they're ready to swim."

"What about first marriages?" I said. "Our husbands traded in two amazing wives like us, only because they could afford it."

"Their reason for getting distracted is their business, not ours," Sharon said. "When you wish him well and keep doing what's best for you and your children, starting a new life can be a great adventure."

Though intimidated by Sharon's dating tips, her other advice resonated with me and made my heart purr that day, and whenever I remembered it in my quiet moments alone. Because when I silently wished Walter well and I thought about doing what's best for me and our children, I was free of anger and fear. I was content, and that was enough.

Also in those quiet moments, I discovered that I wanted to make more choices and friends who made my heart purr instead of hurt. *So why didn't I do that when I chose my first date?*

Because a lightning bolt drew a hulking younger man to me across a crowded singles bar that Sharon took me to. With my spine tingling as he gave me a glass of champagne, I must've sensed he was trouble when I asked him, "What's your biggest flaw?" The gist of his reply inspired lyrics for my song about him, **Love Outlaw—**

> **When talk of love can't be denied, I've gotta run. I've gotta fly.**
> **I make it clear right from the start. I'll always be a thief of hearts.**
> **I'll always play. I'll never stay. I'll never change my bad boy ways.**
> **If you hang with me, enjoy the ride with a Love Outlaw who never lied.**

What was I thinking when I did the flying—right into his arms? Was I up for some trouble to distract me from divorce court? Did I want to un-bond from Walter the same way he'd un-bonded from me?

No matter the reason—if any—behind my succumbing to this big attraction, I eventually noticed a big love-lesson was attached to it like a bow. During our weekly motel room romps, my *Love Outlaw* showed me I also could love sex without loving my partner, until I felt the side effects of *hooking up*, as he called it. That fleeting pleasure was as nourishing as catching a fish, throwing it back, and going to bed hungry.

After a couple months of being gratified instead of satisfied, I threw him back into the dating pool and tried a no-sex diet, using The Lunch Bunch for my experiment.

I'd joined that matchmaking service, which during the past three years had arranged over a hundred blind dates for me over lunch, and I'd met some wonderful men with similar interests and life experience. But lightning hadn't struck again, for me at least. That's why my lunch dates rarely led to dinner. Not that I wasn't asked.

My first year of carnal fasting flew by because I felt satisfied by school activities, Jade's music, Logan's hockey and my own writing, painting and volunteering to produce fund-raising events for local nonprofits. Sharon often fixed me up with her ex-boyfriends so I could join her table at black ties and dinner parties.

No lightning bolt—no second date.

It wasn't until Logan left for college and Jade was fully booked with music and high school activities that I felt my untapped mother love seeping out of me as if through a hole in my soul. In my lonesome nights, I grew hungry for another full-meal deal like I'd had with Walter. I kept wondering, *How do I break my carnal fast?*

When I told my single friends from Chicago and Santa Fe, my tribe of blondes, that I couldn't cross the bridge from platonic to romantic love, we gathered on the mountain as we often did. To observe the third anniversary of my divorce on Columbus Day, I hiked up a Sangre de Cristo mountain trail in northern New Mexico to ask for new love, arm-in-arm with my tribe of blondes.

It wasn't a hair color that drew us together, although many of us were blonde. The Tribe evoked a kind-hearted, enthusiastic spirit that united us and fueled our adventures in loving and living our dreams. Since we're all born with that joyful spirit, the secret is to keep it alive, often with a little nudge from the Tribe.

In that spirit they led me to a log bridge, which had formed when a fallen tree had lodged across a narrow gap. Then they asked me to cross it.

Arms folded, I shook my head, as I had on the first two anniversaries of my divorce. Then I gave them the same old excuse, "I'm scared of heights."

Sharon Milton put her calming hand on my shoulder. "You're afraid of falling from a great height, the way you loved and lost Walter."

"We always took the long way up. He said we had nothing to prove," I whined.

"He was scared to cross," Sharon said with a haughty cackle.

My daughter, Jade, put her arm around me, "We don't care if you cross. See you at the top."

Pressure's off. I still want to cross. As everyone lined up single file, I stood back.

Our energetic, 70ish leader named Nonnie walked up to me. "Feel your fear and take it with you as you cross," she said as she led the others over the log.

Nonnie and Sharon crossed with ease, followed by Jade, and her tribal twin, Sarah (both newly 17). Sarah's mother, Karly Woods, stayed beside me, while her mother, Nonnie, motioned for us to follow.

Hmm. I want to leap over blocks to loving again, and they'd said this would help. Go for it, Hadley girl. I took two baby steps onto the moss-covered log. Then I made the mistake of looking down at the rushing, rocky stream. It was only a half-tree length below me—but I froze. *What a wimp,* I thought, helpless to go on.

From solid ground on the other side, Jade shouted, "Look at me. You won't fall."

Then Sarah said, "Or jump. It feels like flying."

Damn. I see me falling—failing. My heart wasn't exactly purring when I cried, "Get me a helicopter."

"I'll spot you," Karly said, as she stepped on the log right behind me.

With her added weight, the log wobbled under my feet, and my arms flew out to find my balance. "I'm going back," I yelled. I felt Karly back off the log.

Nonnie didn't give up. "Ten more steps and you're here. You can do it."

Sharon cheered, "Giddy-up, Cowgirl."

As if courage could be inhaled, I took a big breath of my tribe's good vibes. I still couldn't move my feet. Behind me, Karly shouted to the others, "We'll meet you up there."

Music to my ears. When I leapt backwards onto solid ground, I caught my daughter's disappointed gaze. *Oh well. Maybe next year.*

As Karly and I took a shady trail, she patted my back. "At least you got past the stage when you couldn't handle a weekend without a man."

"Not any man. The love of my lifetime."

"You idealize him like he's dead," she said.

"To me, he is."

"Amazing, since he still calls you everyday. To make sure you don't move on."

Hmm. Where she sees a problem, I see a solution. I said, "We like to share our children's lives, even by phone. I'd told him if we lost our shared stories, divorce would be like Alzheimers. And he'd agreed."

Karly shook her head sadly. Then she led us up a steep bluff that intersected with the approaching procession to the mountaintop. When they were twenty yards below us on the path, Nonnie waved as she saw me. "Ready to ask the mountain gods for a new man?" she called out.

"Not sure I want one," I said, closer to her.

We merged into a cluster of cowgirl hats and Nonnie said, "You've got to know what you want, want it enough to climb a mountain and ask for it, then give thanks, knowing it's yours."

"It's easier to be alone than to risk loving again," Sharon said, as if taking my side.

"She's not alone," Karly said.

I nodded. *Thanks to them, I won't have to face the rest of my life alone. I should feel grateful, not sad.* I wondered aloud, "Is that what I'm doing? Taking the easy way?"

"Only you can answer that," Sharon said. She gestured toward the path that Jade and Sarah had veered up. Following them up to a rocky perch gave us a clear view of the Colorado Rockies a few hundred miles away.

We were breathing in the beauty of the golden aspens and the warmth of Indian-summer sunshine when Jade lifted her arms and spoke to an unseen presence above us. "Hey, mountain gods. Send us a blaze, and we'll thank you the rest of our days."

I had to chuckle when Jade talked like a budding lyricist, and I translated.

"Did you ask for a kind, handsome young man?"

"Fo-shizzle," Jade said. "Now we wait for the gods to set our fate."

Gently, I corrected her. "The choices we make do that, not the mountain gods."

Sarah shrugged. "They don't exist anyway."

"But the universe does," said Sarah's mother, who spoke to the big blue sky. "Forget about a man for me. Send more film work my way," Karly said.

Next in line, Sharon raised her gaze, "Send a buyer for the gorgeous house I renovated."

All eyes turned to me. *I didn't come to the mountain to ask about my career goals.* Looking up at our big sky, I said, "I'd like to love again, like I loved Walter. Or better."

Jade leaned toward me. "What about Judge John? He likes you a lot."

Shaking my head, I said, "He's a dear friend."

"Friendship's good, Mom. You'll just be growing old together."

The women groaned. "Jade honey," I said. "I'd like to burn out in a blaze, like these Aspens in October."

The girls groaned and Jade said, "You're not having sex, are you?"

"Not now. I'm waiting for the lightning bolt of passion I felt with your dad."

"That's janky." Jade's tone meant *weird*.

"Just wait," I said. "There are so many wonders ahead for you girls."

"For all of us," Nonnie added. She sipped her bottled water, and we opened ours.

Karly turned to her mother. "Do you want another mountain man?"

Nonnie shook her head. "I've loved some fabulous men. Enough for now."

"Then what's your wish?" Karly asked.

Embracing us with her smile, Nonnie announced, "I wish you'd all go out there and break your heart like I did."

"I'd like to protect my kids from a broken heart," I said.

Nonnie shrugged, "Then you'll have to live forever."

Jade surprised us. "We all die, so love hurts. Right?"

"But we love anyway," Nonnie said. She put her arms around the girls and resumed the hike and her advice. "We love with every cell in our body. And we forgive. That's what we came here to do, ladies."

"So I should thank Walter for plenty of chances to do both," I said.

Jade turned around. "You talk about Dad, but he never talks about you."

"His wife would slug him," Sharon said.

I'd like to slug her for mentioning what I've tried to forget:

A few days after the first anniversary of our divorce, Walter had called me with news he'd broken up with Tina. "I'm a hundred-percent done with her," he'd said. "Divorce doesn't have to last long. Any chance we could be a family again?"

"Maybe," I'd responded with a touch of malice. "After I love and leave someone new. Then we can talk."

I'd like to forget that my childish me, too, attitude was the final barrier which kept our family apart. If I hadn't shut that door on Walter, he never would've met Marcy or married her the same weekend Logan left for college. How could I have been such a fool?

"I won't mention you-know-who again," I promised.

Jade rolled her eyes, like she didn't buy it. Then Sharon said something she'd told me before. "When you can cut Walter out of your thinking, you'll be free to love again."

"Go for it," Jade said. "I hope we're both in love by Christmas."

My heart purred during the rest of our hike. With Jade's blessing, I was officially free to forget her father and fall for a *Mountain Man*.

The first candidate was waiting at Albuquerque Sun Port a few hours later, when Jade, Sharon and I arrived at a crowded gate for our flight home. Sharon pointed him out to me—the pony-tailed, six-packed young man, who was watching Jade look for an empty seat. He quickly removed a newspaper from a chair, so she could plop down next to him.

From my seat across the aisle, I watched that baby Antonio Banderas admire Jade's honey-blonde hair, her dancer's posture and beaming smile.

I bet he can't see her giggle waiting to erupt, like I can.

As soon as he boarded the flight in the group ahead of us, Jade giggled blissfully. "Can you believe it, Mommy. He's a blaze UNM student going to Chicago to work at Fermi Lab."

"Those mountain gods work fast," I said.

"But he's 24. A little too old for me, and way too young for you."

"Some young guys want experienced women like us," Sharon said. "How old was your Love Outlaw?"

I was upset she'd mentioned him, after she'd told me to keep my dating life private:

"Kids don't want to watch their parents date," she'd said, "so don't bring up or bring home a man unless he's marriage material. And he <u>never</u> sleeps over if the kids are home."

Glaring at Sharon, I said, "Age wasn't an issue."

Jade nudged my arm. "Your love outlaw?"

Hmm. What does she need to know at her age? "It's my song about a man who runs from love, no matter how wonderful his lover is."

Jade scrunched up her face. Then she led Sharon and me to the wall of windows with a big view of the Sandia Mountains. "Hey, mountain gods," she said. "Please send a kind, handsome, loyal guy our own age for each of us to love. And he should say *Mountains* right away, to show us he's *The One*."

Raising her hand, Sharon said, "Give me five."

"Don't be greedy," I said, ending our Columbus Day getaway with a laugh.

The second candidate appeared at our front door six weeks later. On the night before Thanksgiving, the doorbell rang unexpectedly. Jade and I raced to answer it to find snow flurries swirling around an elderly, rotund man, who presented a giant bouquet.

"Frankie's Flowers brighten your day," he said, in the tone of those TV ads.

"For me or my mom?" Jade asked.

Looking at a printed label, he said, "They're mountains of mums for your mum."

"*Mountains!*" Jade shrieked, while I happily gave him a handful of singles.

"I thank you, and so does my wife of 45 years," he said, retracing his snowy footprints to the delivery van.

Jade followed me back into the kitchen, asking, "How'd he get a wife your age, if he's not rich?"

Unveiling a rose-hued bouquet of mums, I said, "After 45 years of marriage, he still sees his wife as his bride. Right attitude for a Mountain Man."

Jade swiped the note card and read out loud. "*My dearest Hadley. Thanks for bringing out the best in everyone who loves you, including me. John.*" Jade looked me in the eyes. "That flower guy said *Mountains* to tell you John's *The One* for you."

Time to give her a chemistry lesson. "The instant I met your dad, I felt a thrill that lasted twenty-five years. I still haven't felt it with John, after six months."

Jade twirled a strand of her hair, a sign she was nervous. "Don't things move slower when you're old? Not that you're old." She turned to the snack drawer, staring vacantly.

"What's bothering you?" I asked.

She grabbed a handful of carrots from the mound I'd chopped for dinner and said, "What will you do when I leave home, and everyone's left you?"

Whoa. That could start a pity party. Gently, I turned her to face me. "Truth is I used to think like that, and I felt awful. So I changed my thinking. I'm excited about having my adventures when you leave home for yours. And I hope you'll be excited for me, too." Jade looked doubtful. "Until then, grab a knife and start chopping. That's when my best ideas come. Another benefit of stir-fry."

On the third Thanksgiving Day after my divorce, I reached an uncomfortable crossroads with a potential *Mountain Man*, and it dimmed the joy of the few hours I had with my children before they spent the holiday with their dad. Snow had delayed Logan's flight home from college until after two in the morning, but that didn't stop us from joining 8000 neighbors in the 8 a.m. *Turkey Trot*—a three-mile run that raised enough money for another year of hot meals at the county shelter so nobody would starve.

Logan and Jade dropped me off in the pokey pack in the rear so I wouldn't hold them back. I admired their energy, which a mere four hours of sleep hadn't diminished.

When a gunshot started the stampede, I stumbled back in time. *I miss the years Walter trotted by my side. The way he'd sleep by my side. The mound of pillows I hold onto every night is a sorry substitute for Walter.*

As usual, that kind of thinking made my heart clench, so I started to think about my blessings. *Great kids and friends. Good health, when my heart isn't clenching. Two cozy homes. A caring co-parent in Walter. Next time he calls, I'll thank him for staying by my side as a parent.*

Near the finish line, I heard a familiar voice call out to me. "Want some company?" John trotted up to me from the sidelines. He was bundled in a parka with a tied hood and scarf. I'd already peeled off my outer gear.

Guessing his strategy, I said, "You want the glory, without working up a sweat."

"Busted." John and I crossed the finish line together at 38:43. I saw my children cheering in the crowd of well-wishers who'd finished long before we did.

"Good job," Logan said. I fit neatly beneath the arm he put around me. The smoky scent of chilled sweat reminded me of his many boy-hugs after he'd played outside on crisp fall days.

Jade squeezed into our huddle. "Family hug."

John tried to fit into our family circle. "I'm glad we're all here, so I can ask you kids an important question."

"Shoot," Logan said. He finished his post-race apple and tossed the core in a can.

"You know I think your mother's amazing."

"She's a catch," Logan said, poking me.

"I'd love to be a positive part of your family," John said. "So if you two approve, I'd like to ask your mother to marry me."

Whoa. Do I kiss him or kill him? Without waiting for the approval he requested, John knelt before me. Curious trotters gathered around us, and I whispered, "Not now, John." But that didn't stop him.

"My dearest Hadley. With your children as witnesses, I promise to cherish you and do whatever I can to make you happy for the rest of our lives. I'd be forever honored if you'd marry me. Will you? Marry me?" He finished with a hopeful smile.

Spectators whistled. I dropped to my knees, prompting a hush in the crowd. I looked at my children, who nodded encouragement. I looked back at John.

"That's really great. Wow. Well…I love that you're crazy enough to ask me in front of the whole world. But—" After stammering my thanks and admiration, I realized what I truly wanted. "Your honor. I'd like a continuance."

I saw the glimmer of hope drain from John's face, from my children's faces, and from the entire circle of faces surrounding us. I stood up and started to pull John up from his knees, but he pulled away from me.

That evening, during our Thanksgiving feast for two at my festive dining room table, I dreaded his inevitable follow-up question, which he'd graciously withheld until we finished our main course. "How long of a continuance do you need, Hadley?"

Do I jump at the chance to marry a wise man, devoted dad and caring friend now, and learn to love him later? Hmm... "I need time to see if I could love you the way you deserve to be loved. The way you seem to love me."

"How much time?" he asked.

"I can't say. But we'll know when it's right for both of us."

He seemed to be delaying a response by carrying the china and silver into the kitchen. "If your ex took the kids overnight once in a while, we'd be married by now."

"After six months of dating?"

"Plenty of time for most adults, with regular overnight bonding."

It was my turn to delay. I carried our wine into the vaulted family room, set two cushions on the floor by the fire and sat down. "That's not an option."

He sat down next to me. "Because Walter still controls your life."

I cringed, but avoided a debate. "I could've arranged overnight coverage if I'd wanted to."

John adjusted his glasses like he did when he was about to ask an uncomfortable question. "So it wasn't logistics?"

How do I soften the truth? "Maybe I'm like a bottle of red. I need to breathe before being drunk."

"I hope you do more than that. I hope you let yourself love again."

"I'm waiting for the lightning bolt that hit Walter and me at first sight." I felt sorry for him as I watched his cheeks flush with frustration.

"You're not twenty anymore. At our age, love isn't a BAM. It's an Ahhh. So open up and say, Ahhh."

Though flattered by his persistence, I sensed beneath his words a bullying need to do things his way. "You say and do everything right. But something in me says, *No. Wait.* I have to trust that."

He gazed at the fire for a few breaths before he turned to me, "I'll miss you."

"You're still invited for dinner."

He looked at me as if he were memorizing my face. "Dinner's not enough."

What if I'm making a big mistake? What if like can turn into love? "I'm writing a song about friendship catching fire. That could happen, if we give it time."

He rubbed his eyes and sighed. "I'm not a patient man. So I won't see you again. Unless you or your kids have an emergency and need my help. I'll be there for you. I hope you know that."

A surge of compassion made me wrap my arms around him. He grabbed me for a hungry kiss, but I gave him my cheek instead of my lips. His disappointed pout was a big turn-off for me, and he noticed. "Both kids are away, but you still won't play."

I shrugged. "We're not a love match."

In the silent void, we watched the fire burn down. When John got up to leave, he suggested we meet in a month. I agreed. But that meeting wasn't the one I'd hoped for.

The next time I saw John was at Sharon Milton's holiday mixer for single friends in the city. I felt a tremor of jealousy when he introduced me to his perky date, Tiffany.

"Sharon set us up after you set me free," John told me with a vengeful smirk.

"He's a great Christmas gift," I told Tiffany, who took his arm and led him away.

Three weeks later, I read of their engagement in the society page. My heart was racing. *How can a sensible man like John be so fickle?*

That night I eased my blues in a bubble bath and went to sleep thinking I was over it. The next morning Sharon called to ask how I felt about John and Tiffany.

"You should've asked me that <u>before</u> you fixed him up with her," I snapped.

"You're pissed at me?"

It's not all her fault. "At him, for snagging the next blonde who wanted to be a Judge's wife."

"I was surprised you passed on a five-star guy. They don't last long."

"No chance for second thoughts, thanks to you."

"I only have one thing to say about that. SOULFULDATES.COM," Sharon said.

She'd been asking me to join that online dating site for the past year, but I was stuck on the edge of that dating pool, afraid to dive in. That's where Sharon had met John. When they didn't click, she'd introduced him to me, and the rest was history.

Sharon insisted, "You should sign up while I'm at his wedding bash tonight. Did I tell you he fixed me up with his best man?"

"I'm jealous," I shrieked. "Yet I never loved him."

"He's not the only Knight on the site, so get your profile up there tonight."

That was the nudge I'd needed. On that special night dedicated to romance, I sat alone by my fire, sipping Merlot and trying to see the bright side: *I didn't settle down with a platonic friend. I've honorably freed myself to fall for my Mountain Man. I know he's out there, hoping to find me. How do I help him?*

With no *Mountain Man* in sight on the third Valentine's Day since my divorce, I decided fate wasn't working fast enough. So I fired up my high-speed internet and logged on to find a SOULFULDATE on the world-wide web.

2. ADVENTURER WANTED

"Adventurer wanted. Share meals and miles
Sunrise. Sunsets. Sorrows and smiles
Rise again, plowed down by pain.
Become all that we might have been.

"I wrote a song called 'A Change Of Heart' to ask for
a new love, after my long, passionate marriage ended in
divorce a few years ago. I've enjoyed a creative rebirth
and feel ready to love freely and deeply again.

"Are you a man of your word who seeks chemistry,
communication and kindness in a relationship? Are you
free to love and be loved, to know and be known as a
way to keep the magic alive? If so, I'd love to hear from
you. Oh, my name is SONGBIRD."

 I whistled SONGBIRD's CALL. Then I clicked
off my web camera.

That's how I introduced myself on video when I followed Sharon's advice
and signed up for SOULFULDATES.COM. Jade had showed me how
to use a web cam we'd attached to my computer before she went to Cupid's
Hip Hop dance at her school.

"Change out of your mom clothes and use some blush," she'd said.
"You'll look like your TV days."

When she danced out of my office, I took her advice. In honor of the
third Valentine's Day since my divorce, I slipped into a red dating dress, a
slinky two sizes smaller than my married clothes I'd given away to a
women's shelter while the ink was drying on my divorce decree.

"Stress becomes me," I'd often said whenever friends noted how much weight I'd lost during my breakup.

With that stress long gone, a little exercise and a lot of whole foods helped me stay in shape. That's why I decided to pay ten bucks more each month for face-to-face video chats with potential SOULFULDATES, "without Big Brother monitoring live broadcasts between members," their website advertised.

I liked the idea of video chats for many reasons.

Luckily, the camera was still my friend, having worked in front of and behind it in local television for nine years after college, before I took a sabbatical to raise my children.

During a video chat, men could see how I looked at midlife and decide if they wanted to see more. That worked both ways. If I didn't like a man's looks, his voice, or what he had to say in his video, I didn't have to contact him.

"What if nobody contacts you?" A part-time nurse named Dolly doused my excitement over online dating the next morning, after I told my tribe of spinners at our neighborhood gym what I'd done the night before. While nearing the end of a nine-minute climb on our stationary bikes, Dolly dried her face and continued. "You may be on a hunt for a man, but what if nobody hunts for you?"

Whoa. Could that ever happen? Hmm. "I could send a good prospect a smiling Buddha icon to let him know I'm interested."

"Buddha?" Kabir, a surgeon from India and the only man in this Tribe shook his head. From the next bike, his wife and medical partner named Meeka, tapped his hand.

"Is he a reminder to stay awake to love?" she asked.

I watched Kabir nod and give his wife a smile that made me smile.

Dolly guzzled some water and framed her advice gently. "Without a chase and conquest, a man won't value you as a prize catch. So you don't hunt for a man."

Our 20-ish spinning leader named Kimba stood up on her bike, which faced us so we could watch her perfect body rain puddles on the floor. "My mother says I should go for a boy who can't live without me and learn to love him," Kimba said. "Should I sign up for a SOULFULDATE?

"Why not?" I said.

From her bike next to mine, Dolly swatted my arm with her towel. "You think you can compete with a fresh look like that?"

Do I remind her that Walter ended up with a lovely woman his own age, with similar life experience and core values? Or would that sound too preachy? "So if nobody comes drooling after me, I'm only out one night to write my application and a couple hundred bucks to join for a year."

Kabir didn't sound preachy when he said, "An arranged marriage with someone who shares your values and goals is stronger than a match based on silly notions about hunters, the chase, physical beauty and romance. Right, Dear?"

His wife nodded. "That works for us, but not for home-grown Americans. Do you agree, Hadley?"

"I don't know how this works. When I figure it out, I'll let you know," I said, although I secretly vowed to keep my dating discoveries private, after their concerns had made me sweat. Since I usually sweated discretely, in my armpits only, I sensed the beads of sweat on my forehead were beads of fear: *Would any hunters seek a woman like me, when girls like Kimba were vying for their attention?*

I waited 24 hours before I had the nerve to find out. While Jade and three teenage boys in her band played their rumbling music in our basement before dinner, I logged on to see if any hunters had contacted me.

With my yellow lab, Lily, snuggled at my feet, and my love, Merlot, in a goblet on my desk for moral support, I learned there was nothing to fear. Several hunters had contacted me. The first was a shaggy, Howard Stern look-a-like, minus his sense of mischief:

"Hi SONGBIRD. I'm BREWEDAWAKENING. I bet we could make beautiful music together if you buy coffee, produce and chocolate with a "Fair-Trade Certi-fied Label", so farmers are fairly compensated. Do you

stick to grass-fed meats, and avoid products made in unsavory conditions abroad? If you're also carbon neutral, or even know what that means, let's wake up and smell the coffee together. OK? Please reply soon. Waiting will be torture."

Hmm. He could get me inching toward activism, if he had some pizzazz. How shall I end his torture? I activated my web cam and said:

"Hi BREWEDAWAKENING. It's SONGBIRD, but I guess you see that. Anyway, I admire your path and know I could learn something from you. But I'm not responding in ways that could connect us as a couple. Your SOULFULDATE's still out there, hoping you find her. Happy hunting."

I clicked on my next video from a blond kid about Logan's age, wearing a t-shirt, torn jeans and pointy leather boots. He sounded nervous as he said:

"Hi SONGBIRD. BEMYBOSS. If you'll boss me around, I'll clean, cook, and run errands for you. If you use a whip when I'm bad, I'll pay you for my room and board. OK?"

Do I tell him I didn't spank my own kids, and I'd catch him being good so often that he'd become a new man? Is that what he wants to hear?

I said:

"Bad timing, naughty boy. I already have a devoted housekeeper."

My next hunter sat on a beach, flexed his tanned chest and made me grin:

"Hi SONGBIRD. It's I'MNOTADOCTORANDI-DON'TPLAYONEONTV. Actually, I'm a Nobel laureate who developed the internet with Al Gore. I was Mr. America and won four gold medals in the 63rd Olympiad. If anyone can beat that, you definitely should date him.

Just kidding. But if you're looking for a regular guy who's respectful, honest and loving, I'd love to hear back from you. Why? Well, I bet you can work a room of stuffed shirts and walk on my Naples beach in a bathing suit. Want to join me? If not, tell me why—if you do reply."

I bet I still had a big grin on my face as I activated my web cam and said:

"You're a charming guy, but your Naples home base doesn't work. I'll be living near Chicago until my youngest child leaves for college. Good luck finding your SOULFULDATE."

I thought I'd closed the door, so I didn't expect his instant reply:

"Hi, SONGBIRD. I can conduct my business from any computer in the world. I'd brave Chicago winters if I could warm up with you."

Since I had no desire to *Giddyup*, I had to say *Whoa*:

"I'm flattered. If I were connecting to you differently, I'd probably ask you to buy the house next to mine. But I can't encourage you to move here on my account. Although you'd meet many wonderful women like me here, if the spirit moves you this way. Happy trails."

"How do you avoid stalkers, Mom?"

That made me jump. My ears had started ringing in the stillness after Jade's band stopped playing, but I didn't expect to see her standing there.

"No need to worry," I said. "There's nobody I've wanted to meet in person."

Jade glanced at the flexed profile on my computer screen. "I can't tell if that old guy is hot, but he's smart if he wants to date you."

"It's not dating. It's meeting. Nobody said *Mountains* yet."

She smiled and said, "The guys have homework"—my cue to serve our plates and sit down to dinner with the band. *It's nice to have men at the table again.*

Like a child who bolted to the Christmas tree to discover gifts Santa left the night before, I woke before dawn the next day and looked for messages from hunters. Two had arrived during the night. The first was from a masked man, whose web cam drifted down from his ZORRO mask down to his open shirt, dangling red tie and erect silhouette:

"Morning SONGBIRD. I'm BJ9-IN. I'll buy the cocktails and let my instrument keep you singing all night. Could you handle nine inches?"

So that's what happens without monitoring members. Bad pun. I stopped his video and blocked him from contacting me again. *Thankfully, Jade didn't see that one. Do I dare click on the next one?*

I didn't get the chance. My phone rang and I was called to substitute for the Drama Teacher who had the flu. For the next three days, I forgot about hunters while I helped middle-school students in a private school rewrite and rehearse original one-act plays for staging the following week.

Their regular Drama Teacher emailed me after he saw the results: "Great work, Mrs. Finch. You're a tough act to follow."

I loved being a mentor, although after a few days in the classroom I was glad to get back to work on my first novel, which was about the adventures in starting fresh and loving again. Since my life was short on adventures lately, my writing was slow moving. That's when I remembered my latest creative outlet.

Before dawn, I logged onto SOULFULDATES.COM and was struck by the rugged good looks and intriguing inquiry from a top candidate for my *Mountain Man*:

"Hi there, SONGBIRD. I'm JOURNEYMAN and I'm curious about you. If serenity is determined by how often you feel disturbed, are you as serene as you seem?"

Wow. A hot man who looks beyond the surface.

"Hello, JOURNEYMAN. By your definition, I'm very serene. Hopefully not in a boring way, but in a fun, caring way. I used to be very disturbed by my breakup, but I've learned to see each challenge as a chance for positive change. Is that how you see things? I hope so, because you're the first man I've been attracted to on here. I hope that didn't scare you off."

I clicked on his video bio and noticed JOURNEY-MAN was ONLINE NOW.

I was thrilled to receive his instant request for an interactive chat:

"Truth time, SONGBIRD. When was the last time you lied, and why?"

"I listed the age I look instead of my actual age when I signed up here."

"What was your darkest lie?"

He's already looking for character flaws. Was he burned by a liar?

"Disarming question, JOURNEYMAN—I can't recall a dark lie. Not that I haven't made some big mistakes. But I usually blab them, so I'm more of an open book than a Mata Hari. Did you ever make a big mistake?"

His voice took on a serious tone:

"Dearest SONGBIRD, Though I was happy in my marriage and never intended to stray, I started confiding in a woman at work and we fell in love. For six months. My big mistake was confessing to my wife, who left me and took our children with her."

"I'm so sorry for you and your family, JOURNEY-MAN. Maybe your mistake was sharing intimate details of your life with another woman. That steals your focus from your wife, which is as big of a betrayal as your first extramarital kiss. Not to judge, but what you lose focus on, you lose."

As I waited a minute for his reply, I felt uneasy. *Did the truth turn him off? Or was it my pink flannels? Damn. I also forgot to wash my face. What happened to my vanity?*

I darted out of my office, intending to get dressed, when I heard the beeping of a video-chat request. *Do I talk to him or worry how I look?*

I raced back to see what he had to say:

"Here's my thinking, SONGBIRD. If we were a couple, I'd stay faithful to nurturing our soul growth, including all experiences outside of our relationship this might entail. Could you get to this point on my path?"

My heart clenched, and gave me my answer:

"That fork in the road would tear us apart. **So I'd choose passionate monogamy again, since that never hurt me or my family."**

"If you have A Change Of Heart, let me know."

I liked his gentle persistence, but I wanted to run from his path. I replied:

"Happy trails, JOURNEYMAN."

When we disconnected, it felt like a breakup, but we'd never actually met. I didn't want to think about my dashed hopes, so I bundled up and took my 13 year-old yellow lab for a walk. Splashing in the melting snow, Lily looked up at me, as if to ask for approval to get soaked. I removed her leash. She dashed toward the creek beside our house, looking proud she still had what it took to chase away a flock of geese.

Near her slushy paws, a purple patch caught my eye: The first crocuses of spring, blooming through melting snow. I wondered, *Is our beauty wasted, if no lover sees? Yuck. Flip the switch fast.* I grabbed my pocket notebook and wrote:

No beauty's wasted when you bloom for you
All beauty's tasted when you bloom for you

Love your wildflowers, dandelions, too
Bloom for you. Bloom for you.

Tucking away my notebook, I felt content to bloom for Lily and me.

At eight the next morning, I was back in the classroom to sub for the Language Arts teacher who'd also caught the flu. When I asked her fifth graders to continue writing essays for the class magazine, they complained it was *way too much work.*

Time for a gentle nudge. "We each have two choices every day: Grow seeds of greatness that let your talents bloom. Or let weeds of laziness choke your blooms. Who wants to be generous with your talents and make it a great bloomin' day?"

They all did, some more eagerly than others. I knew it might not have been that easy to get them on task, if this weren't a school for talented children whose seeds of greatness had been lovingly nurtured since they arrived on this planet—my wish for all children.

My wish for a SOULFULDATE: When I clicked on the site that night, I added another ideal trait in my dating profile:

I'd like to meet a man who'd nudge me into greatness like I would for him. Could that be you?

"Hello, SONGBIRD. I'm AGREATGUY4U. Liked your song lyrics in your profile, and I want to know more. Do you have an album I could buy?"

I took my web cam and showed him boxes with 2000 unsold albums stacked around my home office, and then I sent him to the only place it's sold—on the internet via CDBABY.COM.

A week later, I heard back from this mid-20's man with a fresh grin:

"Hey, SONGBIRD. Remember me? AGREAT-GUY 4U. I got your album. I'd like to know what you

know about love. Teach me?"

He looked like an earnest boy scout seeking his next merit badge. I had no desire to date a *son figure* or alienate a young man who bought my album, so I replied tactfully:

"My album starts with lost love and ends in the *Fire Of Love*. Isn't that where we all want to be? I hope you experience that joy. Best of luck in your search for a SOULFULDATE."

Two-dozen men contacted me during my first few months on that site, but I never felt a *Bam* or an *Ahhh* of attraction, as John had called it. Nonetheless, I instantly saw the benefits of using the dating site as a networking tool.

I started selling more albums to interested SOULFULDATES than had been sold during my pricey radio airplay campaign with an L.A. company, which had gotten three of my songs spinning on dozens of AA radio stations from Maine to Maui.

Unfortunately, that radio airplay hadn't increased record sales, since radio DJs never told listeners how to buy my album online. I was the only one giving that info to men who wanted to go out with me.

After a SOULFULDATE told me he listened to my album, I invited him to meet for coffee and a pastry at Joyful Cafe as thanks for his support. My treat, in many ways. As we traded love stories, I felt a fond connection with the men who bought my album—twenty men in three months, while my sales doubled to a whopping 46.

At that sales rate, it would be decades before I recouped a big chunk of my divorce support, which I'd used to record my first album. *Oh, well. At least I enjoy my meetings to share old love stories. When will I start a new one?*

I quickly realized that wouldn't happen with my next SOULFULDATE named LIVINGLARGE. A muscular man of 55, his wrinkles looked more rigid in person, sitting across from me in a cozy corner of Joyful Cafe. He seemed agitated and oddly silent. I found out why, when he reached into his jacket and slammed chunks of my CD on the table.

"That's for man haters like you," he said. "I hated your first song."

That song was **Value of a Woman**—

> What's the value of a woman who pours love on every
> chore?
> What's the value of a woman who sees my flaws and
> loves me more?
> What's the measure of her song that fills our hearts
> with harmony?
> I learned the value in the pain she caused on the day I
> set her free.

In that song, I wrote about regrets I'd imagined Walter felt over our breakup. He never told me this, but I felt better writing it. Somehow it triggered this man's rage. I wanted to run. Calmly, I told him, "Each song's a canvas. You paint your own feelings on it."

Under his breath, he called me a *female dog* and left. Although I was relieved my cafe witnesses were there to keep his anger from escalating, it still made me tremble like aftershocks of a quake. *Like my angry outbursts with Walter had shaken me. Was that why LIVINGLARGE came to me? To show me the old me? To remind me how I could forgive myself for all the times I showed up in anger and hurt my husband and myself? My heart purred, a sign that was a good way to look at it.*

As I left the cafe, I silently thanked LIVINGLARGE, my living mirror, for showing me why I signed up for a SOULFULDATE. And it wasn't to sell albums.

Have you learned from lost love? And have you let it go?

Are you willing to change? Willing to grow?

And if you see the best in me, let's go tenderly.

Don't wait, come on, write a new love song with me.

Come to me. Let's fall in love.

Leave your fear. Bring your tears, come to me.

Come to me. Let's fall in love.

Don't play it safe. Take a leap of faith, baby. Come to me.

3. COME TO ME

Once again, I fine-tuned my portrait of an ideal **SOULFULDATE** in new lyrics and shared a few bars as my new intro for my dating video. That may be how I attracted an intriguing prospect:

"Hello again, SONGBIRD. I'm your man, JOUR-NEYMAN. Will you Come To Me in the mountains, if I send a plane for you?"

Mountains! Whoa. I'd be heading for heartbreak with him.

"I'd love to. But I'm still resisting your path, JOUR-NEYMAN. My loss."

"My loss. Can't you date without worry over outcome?"

"I was married so long. I guess I know how to love—not how to date."

Hmm. A seed for a song? I made a note, as I watched his reply:

"**Nobody knows how to date. I'd hoped for fireworks, but I'd settle for a fire and separate bedrooms. Fly to me, SONGBIRD?**"

His playful grin and gentle laugh lines were hard to resist.

"**I'm tempted but I can't fly on a whim 'til I'm empty nested next year.**"

I knew my *custodial parent excuse* wasn't fair to Walter, who'd offered to stay with Jade if I ever wanted to be away for a few days. I withheld my real excuse: When I fast-forwarded to our *fork in the road*, my heart clenched. A sign it wasn't ready to be broken again. Unfortunately. So I politely declined his invitation and resumed my search a few days later. I was glad I did.

"**What's a nice girl like you doing on a site like this?**"

I recognized the chiseled cheekbones and haughty voice of my date for a few black ties right after my divorce. With Marcus McKinley I'd felt the potential for a lightning bolt, but it hadn't struck yet. Luckily, I hadn't changed into my P-Js before I replied:

"**Three years without a word, and that's your opening line? How've you been, Marcus?**"

"**I'm an ARTISTOFLUV.**"

His arrogant tone made me tease him:

"**You're an ARTISTOFEMPTYBEDSAND-BOUDOUIRS.**"

"**Of lovers who just left, with traces lingering in tussled linens. We never got there. Did we?**"

I groaned quietly, hoping the web cam missed it.

"**You would've remembered. I stopped wondering why you stopped calling.**"

His steel blue eyes softened as he said:

"Sorry, Hadley. I couldn't stand another story about the wonderful Walter. Again, I'm sorry. But I knew we shouldn't date 'til you were divorced a year or two."

Poof. I forgive him so I can talk without whining:

"It's been three years, Marcus."

"And you're still single? You've got *marry me* flashing in your eyes."

He still had a knack for embarrassing me.

"I'm starting to love single life."

"It shows. Your radiance is contagious, SONGBIRD."

"You sound like an ARTISTOFLUV. Tell me more."

Grinning like he acknowledged my green light, he said:

"I will. If you Come To Me for my 50th birthday party Saturday. Bring an overnight bag, just in case."

Ahhh. I felt a warm stirring that could draw me out of my long hibernation. Imagining lusty ways to do so, I said:

"Your big birthday will be a big night for both of us."

As I'm getting older, I've started to see benefits of my fading memory. I've started to forget the bad stuff and remember the good, far more often than I forget where I put my car keys or why I walked into a room.

When I walked into the birthday bash and saw a dozen of Marcus's female friends hanging on his every word, I realized I'd forgotten how his phone calls, gallery openings and dinner dates with gal pals used to bother me when I first met him. Judging by the new knot in my stomach, it still did.

Behind me, I heard, "Giddyup, Cowgirl."

"Hey, Sharon." I gave her a hug and a hostess gift. "Thanks for hosting his party."

"My pleasure." Sharon whispered, "He's a wild ride, so enjoy him."

I'd also forgotten Sharon had dated Marcus for six months before they broke up and she passed him to me. "It wouldn't bother you, if I got involved with him?"

She shook her head. "It's a small town. And I'm in love with one of his friends."

"In love? And I haven't met him yet?"

"In lust. You'll meet him tonight." Sharon parted the sea of Gal Pals and led me up to Marcus. "Hey, birthday boy. Here's the one who got away."

Marcus gave me a big kiss, and his GPs applauded excessively, as if they worshipped him. Lightly stroking my cheek, he said, "You're turning red. Nice shade."

"Thanks to you," I said. *Another knot in my gut. On guard.*

He smiled. "You're so easy to be with. Nothing bothers you."

"If it does, I walk away," I said. "Because I can't change anyone but me."

Marcus nodded like he understood, and then he introduced me to each of his glamorous GPs, beginning with a 50ish pal named Linda. Dressed in a St. John knit dress,she squeezed my hand. "Treat him well, Hadley." Giving Marcus an adoring smile, Linda said, "I hope to hear a good report about her on Monday."

That was odd—like all the eagle eyes watching me. Marcus introduced me to a younger brunette named Debra, with her toned body barely covered by her red sheath.

Debra held my hand between both of hers. "You seem softer than Walter described you," she said. "I dated him right before he met his new wife."

When he shopped his dick around town like the world was about to end? Whoa. Don't let that old anger spoil the new me. Keep things light, Hadley girl.

"We like the same things," I said, savoring their sly grins and giggles.

"We like kama sutra powder and a feather duster with our ARTISTOFLUV," said Suzie, a buxom red-head.

When he bowed like a proud stud and a dozen of his GPs shrieked in delight, I asked the group, "Am I the only one who hasn't slept with him?"

I heard a man's voice say in a playful Bogie tone, "It's you and me, kid."

Looking beyond the sea of GPs, I tossed a *thumbs up* to a silver-haired, sexy man seated by the fireplace, with Sharon snuggling on his lap. *Her new Mr. Lust?*

"That's my old friend, Scott Murphy," Marcus said, and then he guided a flaxen-haired waif toward me. "You've heard me mention Steed," he said. "She flew in to surprise me."

Steed? The damsel in distress he'd rescued financially, a few times, and he'd never had a good word to say about her? Did she bring her overnight bag?

Her hand was limp when I shook it. "Hello, Steed," I said. "How's life in Maine?"

"Chilly." Eyeballing my busty cashmere chest, she crossed her arms over her petite silk chest and announced, "I'm moving here with my kids for school."

Marcus gave me a shrug that said he had no control over that. I challenged him, "What am I doing here?"

"You're a nice, solid woman," he said.

"A man's wet dream," I blurted.

Marcus chuckled. "I was quoting my parents' reasons why you're a keeper. I'm starting to agree, after my crazy rides with city drama queens."

Steed pointed at me. "<u>She's</u> the bland suburban housewife?"

"Apologize," Marcus said.

Steed lifted her chin defiantly. "For what you said about her?"

I like to see him squirm. I bet if we pooled the tidbits he'd confided in us, we'd find out why he broke up with each one of us.

"Is that how you see me?" I asked.

"Bland—like white bread," Marcus said. "Sweet relief after serial wild women."

I'd also forgotten my wild woman, until he pointed it out. "My wild woman's waking up," I said.

"With me?" Marcus asked with a seductive grin.

When every gal pal turned to me, expectantly, I knew how Arthur Miller must have felt when he realized Marilyn had been intimate with every man at a party. In the Arthur role, I lost my desire to *Giddyup* with everyone's ARTISTOFLUV. So I had to say *Whoa*. I was extremely uncomfortable, so I slipped out of there before dinner, without meeting Sharon's new *Mr. Lust*.

Driving South on Lake Shore Drive, I listened to my song that reminded me of other pleasures that won't break my heart in an ***Affair Of Art***—

> **With no one to hold in your drought of the heart**
> **It's time for a wild affair of art**
> **With a writer's pen or a painter's brush**
> **With a dancer's move a creative rush, a creative rush**

When I returned home and heard Jade's band practicing downstairs, my suburban nest never felt so cozy.

"My wild woman's hiding," I announced to my tribe as we gathered in Santa Fe the following weekend. We were on an afternoon trail ride in Diablo canyon—the rocky masterpiece which made you feel part of all the cowboy films that had been shot there for decades. *Hmm. I never saw film shots of those daffodils blooming out of stone.* They made me cringe and I tried not to think about why.

"Who's your wild woman?" Nonnie asked, from her palomino next to mine.

"She gets me to take risks and shoot for the stars," I said.

"Poof," Nonnie said, as if sending me magic dust with her fingertips. "You take risks and shoot for the stars."

"It's that easy to change?" asked Max, lopping in line a couple horses from mine.

Maxine was her full name, but she didn't broadcast that to people she just met, like our tribe. A black news anchor, Max was newly separated from her white cameraman-husband whom she married while we worked together fresh out of college. When she'd called me for advice about her breakup, I'd invited her to spend a weekend with my friends who'd helped me through that tough transition.

"What you see, will be," Nonnie shouted—her words echoed through the canyon.

Max repeated it, like she wanted to remember it. Then she said, "I see your tribe of blondes. I sure don't qualify. But thanks for including me this weekend. My troubles seem small against all this beauty."

Nonnie smiled. "With that attitude, you're an active member of the Tribe."

"Should I dye my hair blonde?" Max asked with a grin.

"Only if that tickles your fancy," Nonnie said.

"It's a spirit, not a shade," I told Max.

"How do you two know each other?" Nonnie asked.

"From our television days," I said. "Before my two babies and her three Emmys."

"I've got Emmys instead of kids' trophies on my TV. Felt I didn't have enough hours in the day for both," Max said.

Karly stole our focus with three words: "I met someone." After our cheers, she said, "Papers are written. Should I file, or not?"

"You've asked us that since Billy moved out," Nonnie reminded her daughter. "If he can't see what he's throwing away after three years, you deserve a fresh start."

Max said, "Three years without *getting some*? Three weeks is too long."

"I've forgotten how long it's been for me," I blurted.

"Then *get some* fast, before you dry up like this damn desert," Max said.

Karly chuckled. "I've been *getting some* with my husband."

"Boundaries, girlfriend," Max said. "He's *getting some more* down the road."

"He says, *No*, but I don't know," Karly said.

"They all say, *NO*," Max said. "My French hairdresser says, *You can fix a broken vase, but it won't hold water.* Don't wait. File. I just did. That's why I'm here."

Do I stop her from making my mistake? I said, "There are big risks if you start dating."

"You've said that before," Karly said.

"If I would've said *Yes* when Walter asked to come back home, we'd be a family forever."

"You are," Nonnie said. "Just living in separate homes."

I shook my head sadly. "What are we doing to our children?"

"Giving them love-lessons they wanted, when they chose us to be their parents before they were born," Nonnie said, as if that were a fact understood by all.

"What are you smokin' around here?" Max sounded like she wanted a hit.

"We see things differently," Nonnie said. "In *The City Different.*"

"So do I file or not?" Karly asked, sounding hot to trot.

"This isn't the time for a yes or no vote," I said. "But I wouldn't get divorced for one date. I'd meet the guy for coffee. If he's not a good fit—"

"*Get some* before you say *NEXT!*" Max said.

"What if she doesn't feel a *BIG BAM* of attraction?" I asked.

"Hey, Charlie." Max poked our silent wrangler on the horse next to hers. "Do guys need a *BIG BAM?* Or will you take a *Little Bam?*"

Shaking his head, Charlie said, "You sound like those Horny Housewives. Want to know how I'd satisfy you, all at once?" Without waiting for a reply, he kicked his horse's ribs. "Hold on, Ladies," he said, as he led us into a trot. When he saw we could keep up, he actually shouted, "Giddyup."

Like it or not, we started cantering like cowgirls, squealing with delight. Looking back at us, Charlie twirled his cowboy hat and yelled, "You're back in the saddle again."

Judging by all the groans as we gathered for dinner at my house, I figured my Merlot was the perfect antidote to our aching bones. Over our first bottle, while a group salad was being prepared, I poached filets of wild salmon and announced, "My kids caught this in Alaska on vacation with their dad and his new family."

"Doesn't that piss you off?" Max asked.

"It's not how I imagined it," I said. "But the more people who love my kids, the better off they'll be."

"She told them so," Nonnie said, sounding proud of me for following her advice.

When the rosy salmon and colorful veggies were presented on hand-painted plates, it looked like we devoured works of art along with our second bottle of wine.

As Max asked to open a third bottle, I said, "Two glasses at sea level are like one glass in altitude."

"Great," Max said, fishing through dirty dishes in the sink. "Oh, corkscrew? Where are you?"

Karly asked me, "Didn't you flip that around?"

"A dyslexic moment." I tried to distract Max from her love, Merlot, by offering her a new pleasure. "Sharon asked me to show you how to use the dating site, since she's in lust with a new SOULFULDATE."

"Soulful lust?" Max asked. Ignoring our objections, she refilled her goblet and ours, while I fired up my laptop and found a message waiting from the most eloquent, astonishing candidate I'd seen on there yet:

> **"Hi there, SONGBIRD. I'm SPIRITRIDER. A strong, caring man. Gentle of hand. Wild in spirit. I am whole and ready to surrender to love in all its beauty. A king, in search of my queen. My ideal woman has a gentle heart. A fiery spirit. She's well read, well versed in the finer things of life, but finds happiness in her heart."**

"That's me," Max and Karly shrieked at the same time, and then did high fives.

I shushed them and pointed to SPIRITRIDER's cherubic face on screen as he said:

> **"Are you mystical? In touch with your goddess nature? Are you a queen in search of her king? I bet you are, SONGBIRD. If so, will you Come To Me?"**

"I'd re-start my engines for him," Nonnie said.

"If he has a brother, sign me up," Max said.

Karly turned to me. "Could you imagine a more perfect *Mountain Man?*"

"Nope. But I can't reply without my web-cam."

"Send him an old-fashioned e-mail," Max said.

"I'll wait for a private meeting when I get home," I said.

On my way to the airport Monday morning, I was squeezed into the appointment schedule for a quick check-up with Doctor G, who'd helped me bounce back when lost-love knocked me down in recent years. The Canadian expat with an Albert Schweitzer brain and Cary Grant charm also combined Eastern medicine practices with molecular health care.

When I walked into his cozy adobe office, Doctor G opened his arms for a hug. "Welcome home, Hadley. It's been a few months, so your heart must be happy."

"It's still clenching." Stretching out on his leather treatment table, I sighed, "Seeing daffodils just triggered it."

He pressed his fingertips on my wrist and read my pulses. "Daffodils upset you?"

My chest tightened at this memory. "They bloomed the day I came home from my mom's funeral, like she was telling me she was part of all this beauty."

"Wasn't that comforting?" he asked, while reading my other wrist pulses with his fingertips.

Why didn't I tell him this before? "She'd said she was afraid she'd die soon. I didn't ask her why. I said she'd never looked better. Two days later, she died in her sleep. Fifteen years ago this week." I swallowed hard. *Feels like yesterday.*

Doctor G placed a comforting hand on my forehead. "How do you love the thoughtless you?" he asked, as if assigning me that task. Then he started muscle testing—*kinesiology*—placing vials of nature's compounds on my belly, pressing my raised arm to see what strengthened or weakened me.

"Your heart needs a good meal," he said. "When it clenches, do you flip the switch?"

I nodded. "I'm too blessed to be stressed. And I can't get a good buzz without a bad hangover. Got an antidote?"

He wrote two extra items on his supplement list and asked to see me in a month.

Thankfully, my vino headache faded during our flight home from Max's intoxicating initiation weekend. That evening, I felt butterflies while I slipped into a dating dress and fired up my web cam for my belated reply to SPIRITRIDER:

"You take my breath away... I don't know what else to say."

Two days of anticipation for a two-second reply? Oh, well. I spoke from the heart. If he can't sense that, then we're not a good match.

An hour later, I heard back from him:

"I like your style, SONGBIRD. I signed up for this service because a friend said I won't find my queen randomly in the world. So I described what I wanted, searched and found you. I love the artistic mind tempered with a gentle spirit. Chaos and drama no longer appeal to me. I'd like a partner to roam the world and enjoy each moment with me. Could that be you?"

It sure could. Luckily, I'd waited for a man who saw beyond the obvious nice, solid woman to discover what the renowned ARTISTOFLUV couldn't see in me. But I see an issue. Could I give SPIRITRIDER what he wants? What do I tell him?

"It would be wonderful to roam the world with the man I love. If that turns out to be you, could you wait a year? That's when my youngest child leaves the nest, and I'll be free to travel again. If that timing is a chal-

lenge because you're ready to go right now, I understand. And I wish you happy trails."

"Don't worry, SONGBIRD. I love challenges, especially when shared. Bring them on! Since I wasn't blessed with children in my twenty-year marriage, it gives me chills that you have two teenagers I might get to know, love and do things with. Tell me about them. And you. Like your real name. Mine's Tommy Rider."

I preferred to call him *SPIRITRIDER*, and I liked it when he happened to call me what I call myself—*Hadley girl*. Since we lived 2000 miles apart, we continued to get acquainted in our virtual world. During video chats throughout the day, I'd read him a song lyric I'd written and he'd make a helpful suggestion. Or he'd tell a joke or share photos of his favorite life moments that usually made me laugh. And I love to laugh.

"Can you fall in love on a computer screen?"

I asked him that one night around midnight. I was crushed by his reply:

"We won't find out. I'm signing off the dating site."

I gasped, "Why?"

"The attraction's too great on my end. I'd like to give you my undivided attention until we can suss things out."

When I knew we weren't breaking up, I felt playful:

"Suss things out? What's that?"

"Take it as a compliment, Hadley girl. Only a few women have caught my attention like you have. Not an easy thing to do, I assure you."

A few days later, SPIRITRIDER sent me a 20-page **LOVE CARD REPORT** from a book by Robert Lee Camp, which used the day and month of our birth (but not the year) and planetary cards from the ancient book of destiny to test our compatibility as a couple.

"It looks good," SPIRITRIDER wrote in his cover letter.

When I peeked at the summary page, it said we'd been together in a few prior lifetimes and we could be meant for each other in this one also. Now that might sound goofy to people outside *the city different*, but not to me. I requested an interactive chat:

"You're right, SPIRITRIDER. It looks good."

"We need to meet, Hadley girl. If you're free this weekend, I could fly in Friday and leave Sunday."

I felt giddy in my reply:

"I'd like to see what feelings arise face-to-face."

"In the unlikely event we don't feel the magic needed for a physical connection, we'll still have fun as friends."

"Pressure's off. See you soon."

The next morning I told my tribe of spinners I was wary of his *magic* comment, when I went back to the gym to get in tip-top shape within the next 48 hours.

I was spinning harder than ever during our five-minute climb, when Dolly said, "Magic Schmagic. Wear a spanx to suck up your winter gut and get him to commit to a relationship right away."

Sucking up my abs while I pedaled, I huffed, "I don't know if I want one yet."

Dolly shook her head. "Hook him before he flies home, or the next babe will. You've got one chance to reel him in."

"I'd like a man to pursue me, like Walter did."

"You're not 22 anymore," Dolly said. "That's your competition. Conniving babes who never let anything keep them from the man they want. Including your ex, remember?"

My blood throbbed in my ears, so I slowed down and sipped some water.

"You're scaring her," Meeka said.

"And I won't act out of fear," I said.

Dousing her forehead, Dolly asked, "Are you content on your own?"

"I was a slow learner, but *Yes*. I'm content on my own," I said proudly.

"Good. That's how you'll end up unless you wake up," Dolly said. "The first woman to close the deal gets the guy. And keeps him on a short leash, so he can't stray."

"Yuck." That was the terse review uttered by Kimba, our perky instructor.

"Love 'em and Leash 'em?" I asked Dolly with an edge I rarely used.

"No leash for you, dear," Meeka told her husband. When Kabir squeezed her hand tenderly, I wondered if Dolly understood their unspoken message the way I did: *This is the kind of loving that lasts*.

While I was painting my toes red that night, SPIRITRIDER called me. "Once I get on that plane tomorrow, you can't throw me back until Sunday."

"What if I never want to throw you back?" I asked, in a burst of optimism.

"Hope so," he said. "Sweet dreams."

That's what I'd hoped for, but life intruded. Lily kept me up most of the night, crying to go outside to pee every half hour. When her whimpering was inconsolable, I drove her to the new urgent care animal hospital—at four a.m.

Nobody else was in the tiny lobby, so the young vet with a kind smile quickly took blood samples and prescribed antibiotics.

"Are you keeping this old girl alive for you or her?" he asked.

"How so?" I rubbed Lily's ears to muffle the news I feared.

"It's killer arthritis," he said. "She's a stoic one."

"She wags her tail every day. Often."

He patted Lily's head. "Because she loves you. Is she eating?"

I nodded. "And begging for more."

"She's not ready to go yet," he said. "You should be prepared."

That's not how I want to start my special day. I was in a daze when I shook his hand, thanked him, and drove home with Lily.

My phone was ringing when we walked in the house. When I was asked to sub for the Language Arts teacher that day, my mind raced to find the best excuse:

Lily needs some TLC. I want to shop for food and fix a meal for SPIRITRIDER. I want to set a formal table and give myself a facial. And I want time for a bubble bath, so I'm relaxed when I pick him up at the airport in twelve hours.

Luckily, I didn't mention any excuses. In a split second, I changed my mind and accepted the assignment—after I glanced at the vet's bill and realized it would take me three days of subbing to pay for an hour-long emergency visit.

That was a wake-up call. With my support money dwindling down next year when both kids were in college, it was time for more subbing and saving. Starting now.

While I taught five classes in grammar and composition, Lily slept on my favorite Navaho blanket inside my hybrid SUV. During my breaks, I gave her some TLC.

Because of the time crunch after school, I simplified my dinner menu. Even so, my shopping and food prep took so long that I only had time to twirl around in the shower and slip into a dating dress before my big moment.

In one hour, my *Mountain Man* would *Come To Me* at the airport. It was a thirty-minute drive. If I left now, I'd get there early.

I yawned. *Do I have time for a nap?*

4. MAGIC LOVERS

A spring drizzle had slowed traffic into the airport, and I thought I might be late when SPIRITRIDER called my cell: "I'm here early, but don't rush," he said. "The second I see you, I'll know if there's magic. If your kiss makes my ears wriggle, my 2000 mile trip will be worth it."

Don't pressure me, Buster. "I'm excited to see you, but I don't expect the same jolt as when I met Walter. When our DNA used a lightning bolt to tell us our combined genes would create healthy babies. That's the procreative force behind love at first sight, according to a new article I read."

He chuckled. "Some magic doesn't age, Hadley girl. We can still hope for that."

If he means the old BAM of attraction that I'd been hoping for, that article had convinced me that was a long shot at this stage of the game. But I'm not up for a debate. My guard's up. I don't want it to be.

When I pulled up to the curb at O'Hare and saw SPIRITRIDER, wearing a dark raincoat and bracing himself against the windy city's winds, I couldn't wait to get closer to him. I must have been beaming my biggest smile when I jumped out of my car for our moment of truth.

Gentle, handsome, kind, happy, sexy—I like him! That's what went through my mind when SPIRITRIDER smiled at me, as our virtual connection became real.

"It's you. It's really you." We took turns saying that to each other, like we'd found someone we didn't know we'd lost. That tender spell was jarred by a blaring whistle of a security guard. We hopped in my car and sped away.

During our drive home, SPIRITRIDER gave me with a small gift box, elegantly wrapped in antique black and gold. "My old sorority colors." *Do I finish my thought?* "A sign of home," I said. He smiled and squeezed my hand.

"Wow," was all SPIRITRIDER said when I turned into the circular drive of my Tudor-style home at the end of a wooded cul-de-sac.

He followed me into the kitchen where I welcomed him with a reserve bottle of red that I'd opened before I left. "I've saved this for a reason to celebrate. You're it."

We clicked goblets and tasted each other's lips. *I'm ready to be drunk like the wine.* I whispered, "You're a lucky man."

He grinned and asked me to open his gift. It was a sterling ring with inlayed stones in the shape of an exotic, prehistoric creature. "I designed it," he said. "It's the only original I kept when I sold my company to a big chain."

"You're giving me your only original?" I asked in amazement.

"A copy of the original. Like a lithograph," he said.

"Oh. Well, I'll think of you when I wear it."

He reached to slide it on my wedding finger, but something made me offer my artistic forefinger instead. "A perfect fit, like everything else I imagine about us," he said.

Wow. I don't want to run. I put my arms around him. "I hope you're hungry." He replied with a kiss. We were warming up to each other when the kitchen timer went off. Grabbing hot pads, I took a sizzling delicacy out of the oven.

"You cooked that after work?" he asked. I nodded proudly. He drew me closer for a meaty kiss.

Forget the duck. Let's go upstairs, I thought. Luckily, I resisted my wild impulse because seconds later I heard Jade open the front door and fling her backpack on the foyer floor.

"What smells so good, Mom?" Walking into the kitchen, Jade stopped abruptly when she saw us. "I forgot you kids were meeting tonight. I'm Jade."

SPIRITRIDER gave her a hearty handshake. "I'm Tommy Rider. It's great to meet you. I hear you're quite the musician and student."

"Pish posh," Jade said, glancing at the meat platter. "How can you eat that duck, when her family's waddling all over our yard?"

I showed her a bowl of veggie salad. "Have some and save some for us."

"Where's Lily?" she asked, scooping salad onto her plate.

"In her bed, so she can't beg."

"I love dogs," he said. "Don't lock her up on my account."

"Lily's 98 in human years," Jade said. "When she eats, she farts."

He grinned. "I'll meet her after dinner."

As we carried our full plates into the dining room and sat down at the table I'd set with my mother's china and sterling, Jade waited until he wasn't looking to give me her *thumbs up* review.

He may have noticed that when he turned to her and smiled. "Did your mother tell you I guide the careers of musicians, writers and artists?"

"We don't talk about her dates." I watched Jade's eyes flash with a bright idea, and then she gestured to the paintings on each wall. "What do you think of these artists?"

"I recognize that Kandinsky. But not that one," he said, pointing to a portrait of an artist with an attentive gentleman watching her paint by an outdoor fountain. Wearing clothes of an earlier era, I thought he might have guessed its creator.

"John Singer-Sargeant," I said.

"My mom painted them," Jade said, proudly.

Ahhh. What a lovely cue. "I've copied the masters at the Art Institute of Chicago for five years."

"Is there anything you can't do, Hadley girl?"

I won't let him fall for a fantasy of me. "We learn by copying a master. In life and art. When will I create an original?"

"You've done that," he said, smiling at Jade. "Here she is."

"He can come back," Jade said, gathering her dishes. "I've got my boards tomorrow." She kissed my cheek on her way out. "Would you make sure I'm up at seven, Mom?"

My mental shift was instant. *I don't have the energy to stay up late with a man I just met and then get up early for Jade. So who gets my attention?* "I'll have breakfast ready at seven," I told Jade, while she clanged her dishes in the sink.

SPIRITIDER whispered, "The apple didn't fall far from the tree."

I accepted his compliment with a kiss. I sensed Jade caught a glimpse, as she walked by, so I pulled away from him. *My mother-wall is up, but I don't want it to be.* I thought it might come down after he segued into a tantalizing topic, while munching a walnut and beet salad:

"Have you ever spent hours or days in a microcosmic orbit, sharing your life force with a man you love?"

Feeling enticed yet scared of the unknown, I let out a giddy, "Whoa. Is that an altered state?"

"It's a state of continuous orgasm that will spoil you forever," he said. "You'll never again be satisfied by an American short hitter."

"I was spoiled by a home run king," I said. "I didn't realize I'd confused great sex with love, until he left me."

He nodded without commenting and refilled my goblet with the last drops of red. When I couldn't stifle a yawn, I apologized. He suggested we get some privacy at his hotel. That invitation gave me a burst of energy, which faded when I introduced him to Lily and she barely opened her eyes.

Driving up to the entrance of his hotel, I let my engine idle. *Now what? Do I stay or go?* I waited for a cue from SPIRITRIDER, who cradled my cheek in his hands.

"I want you in my bed," he said. Then he gave me a kiss that dissolved my mother-wall and woke my wild woman. A blaring horn from a taxi jolted us apart. He opened his car door and hesitated.

"I wish I didn't have to be up for a college-board sendoff," I said.

After traveling 2000 miles to make his ears wriggle, I'm sure that wasn't what he wanted to hear. But he was sweet about it. He opened his wallet, gave me a key to his room and asked me to crawl in with him anytime. When his parting kiss nearly made my ears wriggle, the wild me wanted to pull over and race him upstairs.

What did I do instead? I waved good-bye and drove off, drumming up reasons: *We just met. I'm too tired to tango. I don't look as good with-*

out sleep as I did when I was 22. Or even 42. Then he'd find a young girl, like Walter did.

Damn. I thought that old well of sadness was dry. Why can't I have some fun with a terrific guy? Or can I? I started to make a U-turn, but something stopped me. Exhaustion. *Oh, well. Maybe tomorrow.*

I was up before the sun, doing dinner dishes and preparing a colorful array of brain food for Jade.

"Looks great," she said, taking her seat beside me at the table. "He's a kind, handsome man who likes music and you. So what's wrong with him?"

"Nothing yet," I said. *A scary thought.*

After she left for her boards, I was upset that I felt shaky from only two glasses of red last night. Fortunately, I found relief in Doctor G's supplements and a lingering shower massage, which also gave SPIRITRIDER a chance to catch up on two time zones of sleep.

"I missed my chance, and I feel sad." That's what I told Sharon by phone, while I waited for SPIRITRIDER to call me. "I chickened out. I can't date," I whined.

"If you think you can't, you can't," Sharon said. "The opposite sounds like you. Today's Take Two. Have fun and stop by later so our men can meet."

"Sounds like a plan." I dressed for comfort in a pastel twin sweater set over khakis and Italian walking pumps. *Mom clothes,* Jade often called them.

When I hadn't heard from SPIRITRIDER by ten, I went to his hotel room with my key in hand. Something made me knock, instead of barging in.

"I've been waiting for you." He poked his head around the door and looked both ways down the hallway before he gave me a sly smile. "I'm naked."

I know an invitation when I hear one. I froze and instantly regretted it. He threw on a towel and invited me in.

Whoa. His six-pack scares me. So did Walter's muscular thighs on our first tennis date. Could be a good sign, I thought, as I looked around his suite and felt his eyes on me.

"Why'd you hide your great legs, Hadley girl?"

I was defensive. "I dressed for our trek in the city."

He shrugged. "Could I say good morning?"

When he reached for me, I let him kiss me but I felt nothing. He must've sensed it, because he walked into the next room without saying a word. *What's wrong? Why can't I get closer?*

The spring sunshine inspired us to put the top down on my M3 convertible, which Walter had given me for my birthday a month before he left me. During our breezy drive, SPIRITRIDER rattled off his favorite activities: skiing, scuba diving, kayaking, parasailing, white water rafting and camping where you don't see another human for days. He looked at me expectantly, as if waiting for a correct answer to his test.

"Scuba is the only thing I haven't tried," I said. "Does it count if I only camped in our side yard with my kids and our dog? Walter only camped at the Four Seasons."

He chuckled. "Do you like cold weather?"

"In my sheepskin coat."

"That would crack where I camp in Alaska," he said.

"You should date Rocky," I said, taking a pass on his *extreme sports love test*. *Will he think NEXT?*

For our first stop in the city, he asked me to drive to the boutique area of town. I quickly realized why. He chose an Oak Street shop with sexy mannequins in the window, skimmed the full-price racks and held up a Dolce and Gabbana leather and lace outfit.

Hmm. He wants a Hot Momma instead of a Mom. I'm game.

A tan leather skirt slid on like a glove. Sparkly tights, suede pumps and a lace blouse made me feel eager to unveil the newest new me for him. "So, Henry Higgins?"

"Much better. She'll wear it today," he told the salesgirl with a bare midriff and a fake tan. Gesturing toward me he asked her, "Wouldn't you like to look that great when you're her age?"

I cringed. *Is he thoughtless or mean?* When the tab for his fantasy makeover of me amounted to ten days of subbing, my new affordability gauge, I waited to see if he'd offer to pay, even though I'd have to decline that pricey gift if he did. He didn't.

He gave the bill to me, as if passing out a test. I could've balked at this extravagant purchase, but I liked my new dating outfit and happily paid my own tab.

During our stroll down the magnificent mile of shops, galleries, and corporate castles in the sky, I noticed two younger men eyeing me like a work of art.

SPIRITRIDER poked me, "You'd look great on the back of my motor-cycle."

"Thanks," I said, thinking *Kabir calls them Donor cycles. I'd never get near his bike.*

While we waited to ride the giant Ferris wheel at Navy Pier, he took a few photos of me on his cell phone.

My turn to give him a test. "Does your woman need to look like this all the time?"

"If we lived closer, I'd take you to places where makeup and manicures aren't required," he said. "I bet you still look great au natural."

"Feeling great beats looking great in my book." *If he thinks, Next—I will, too.*

"I'd like to meet you in New Mexico," he said. "We could have some fun when you aren't so focused on being a good mom."

Ahhh. He gets me. "Great idea," I said.

"We'll plan something soon," he said. Then he hugged me like a pal. It smacked like a rejection—one that I'd set up each time I resisted the chance to leap into his arms.

I was in no mood to meet Sharon and her *Mr. Lust* for dinner, so we ate burgers on our own at Billy Goat Tavern. Over ice cream, I framed a reason for my resistance. "Each cell in our body tells us to move forward or not."

"It's fear," he said, folding twenties under our meal tab. "If I caused it, I'm sorry."

"I'm sorry, too," I said.

I dropped him off at his hotel before nine that night. He said he'd take a cab to the airport so I could have a lazy Sunday morning, and I agreed. After a parting peck, I drove off thinking, *Adios, Amigo*.

A few days later, SPIRITRIDER called to tell me that his former girl-friend had threatened suicide if he didn't get back with her.

"Is she the wrong kind of paradise?" I was leaning against my cell phone in bed, reading about the demise of the John Galt rail line in *ATLAS SHRUGGED*. I sensed my connection with SPIRITRIDER was heading in the same direction.

"She's bi-polar hell, but I'm addicted," he said. "I can't get enough of that girl."

"Girl?"

"She's twenty years younger and needs my guiding hand."

"So that's why I couldn't connect with you."

"Sorry, Hadley girl," he said. "But there wasn't any magic between you and me."

"Unlikely, while you're also focused on someone else."

"When I can't take any more of her madness, I might start therapy," he said. "I'd like to learn to love a woman who's good for me. A nurturer like you."

If he needs therapy to value my best qualities, then it's absolutely, positively time to say, NEXT. "Good luck with your girl," I said.

"At thirty, I guess she's not a girl."

"Has she put anyone's needs ahead of her own? A mate's, a child's, a sick or dying parent?"

"She's never even had a pet," he said. "But she pushes my hot button."

If that's all it's about, watch out, Buster. "I've noticed a big attraction comes with a big love lesson," I said. "I'd like to learn from a gentler joy."

"Could I see you again, when it doesn't work out with her?" he asked.

Hmm. The tantric carrot he'd offered me was tempting. But he was stuck in his rescue-a-daughter-figure phase. "We're not a love match."

"That could change," SPIRITRIDER said, still the optimist.

I had my doubts. Though disappointed, I imagined how much worse I'd feel if we'd hooked up before he went back to his suicidal girl friend. I was thankful my fear kept me out of my old **Sea Of Pain**—

> **Dove into his ocean 'fore I could swim.**
> **Saw his emotion more that a whim**
> **His powerful current swept me away.**
> **On a wave of pleasure in a *Sea of Pain***

A week later SPIRITRIDER called me in the middle of the night. He sounded agitated when he told me that his girlfriend took his car to go spend the night with a drummer in an alternative rock band because she felt like it. I could see him doing a similar thing to me, so I felt spared.

"Painful stuff," I said. "Sorry you have to go through it."

He cleared his throat. "I've been thinking about you, and had a friend prepare your birth chart to see what's holding you back from loving. Know what I found out?"

"About our other lifetimes together?" I asked.

"I'm not ruling that out," he said. "But this is just about you. About honoring the wild woman inside you who's been held back too long and needs to come out and play."

He's the second man who's told me that. "Are you telling me this because you want to try again?"

"No. As your friend, I thought you should know that obstacle was determined by the stars the minute you were born," he said. "I'd like you to find the love you deserve, so I'll send you the tape of your reading. What you do with it is up to you."

"I'd be happy to pay for it," I said.

"It's my thanks for our weekend. For being a dear friend."

That felt like my glass ceiling, which was keeping me from my glass slipper, but I accepted it. "That's a thoughtful ending to our love story," I said.

Now that SPIRITRIDER and I had *sussed things out*, I ended my brief sabbatical from SOULFULDATES.COM. As I reactivated my dating profile the next morning, I checked my photo *chatologue* to see if SPIRITRIDER went back on the site:

He's got a new photo. He shaved 10 years off his age. He wants a 25-35 year-old girl who's free to travel the world with him. Why's my heart pounding, if we've moved on?

Fortunately, I was distracted from my disappointment when I was called to sub for the science teacher. That morning, while students glued science fair reports on poster boards, I read an intriguing thesis question:

Since our bodies and our planet each are composed of over 70% water, could we clean up its molecular structure with our thoughts, our music, our words, our feelings, our vibrational energy?

Using a camera that magnified molecules of polluted creek water that had been frozen in test tubes, a boy named Harry presented photographic evidence of how frozen dirty water molecules turned darker when he merely thought of an evil man named Hitler, but they changed into beautiful crystals when he played Beethoven or merely thought the word LOVE. Thusly, Harry had duplicated the test results that a Japanese researcher had reported several years earlier.

"You've shown us how our thoughts and feelings can change our physical world," I said proudly. "Now what will you <u>do</u> with this knowledge, Harry?"

"I'd like to get the whole world to think LOVE for one minute and measure changes in the earth's energy fields-before, during and after," he said.

"Ahhh. Someone needs to wake us up, and it might as well be you," I said. His smile told me he was game.

Inspired by Harry, I thought LOVE while I checked messages on the dating site that night. Only one man had contacted me. He used an e-note instead of a video to introduce himself. I quickly understood why:

"Dear SONGBIRD, If you were blind and deaf, I wouldn't have to wish I were taller, thinner, had more hair, and talked without a stutter, so I could win your heart like your smile won mine. My stutter disappears when I sing songs that I write and record in my base-ment. Your song lyrics in your profile really touched me. What more could your ex have wanted than you? Just wanted you to know that I'm a fan. Musically yours, ISOARWHENISING"

I replied via email:

"I'd love to hear you sing. Would you like to meet for coffee Saturday—so we could trade recordings? Let me know."

I arrived on time for our meeting at Joyful Café. ISOARWHENISING stood up when I joined him and said he was on his sssssssecond espresso. His stature was grand, like his enthusiasm, and delightfully contagious. DDDDivorced three years with sssshared custody of two ch-ch-children under ten, he said he'd bring many gggifts and no bbbaggage to our relationship.

Whoa. How do I clear that up? "I thought we should meet, since we're possibly the only songwriters in the western burbs," I said, giving him my debut CD as a gift.

"Oh." He nodded as if he understood this was a networking meeting, and he got down to business. Since he only had one original demo, he brought along a disc-man with headphones so I could listen to six of his original songs while he watched me.

For twenty minutes, I overlooked some music and lyrics that needed work, and heard his voice soar when he sang until he nearly made my ears wriggle. *Can ears really do that? Or was that SPIRITRIDER's impossible litmus test for love?*

"Your voice is magic," I said. "Thanks for sharing it."

He asked for feedback on his favorite song, in which he'd won the atten-tion of a dream girl when he sang for her in a karaoke bar. When she heard him stutter, she walked out. I assumed it was based on his experience and it was heartbreaking. I didn't want to go there. I told him I'd also set a song in a karaoke bar with a happier ending. When I felt lost, I still felt guided by a kind presence, as I dramatized in **An Angel Brought Me Home Tonight.**

"A couple sh-sh-sshould have things in common."

"You're right." I admired the big risk he was taking, so I said this gently, "Yet I don't see us as a couple."

"You couldn't love me bb-because of mmmy—"

"Because I haven't loved any man since my husband. I've only made friends."

He smiled hopefully. "Could I be one?"

What a tender spirit… "Could I fiddle with your lyrics?"

He nodded, so I gave him a few suggestions and asked to hear the new-improved version whenever he recorded it.

As we said good-bye outside Joyful Cafe, part of me felt uplifted by magical moments in another meeting. Another part yearned for another kind of magic:

Mutual desire. That's what I'm ready and eager to feel again, my dear mountain gods. Haven't I been patient long enough?

5. ROCKET FUEL FOR ADVENTURE

I was reading by the fire, home alone on Saturday night, when I wondered if any hunters had noticed I was back on the site. Checking in by laptop, I saw the observant one:

> **"Welcome Back, SONGBIRD. I'm your man, JOURNEYMAN. I missed your cheerful face on here the past few weeks. Sorry if that means a new love didn't work out for you, but I'm glad you're back. I've been talking to myself about setting some boundaries, and I'd be open to some exclusivity with you. Now would you like to meet me?"**
>
> *Start your engines*, my wild woman purred.
>
> **"My dear JOURNEYMAN, Let's get together for coffee one day next week."**
>
> **"The Palm Wednesday night?"**
>
> I liked having dinner with Jade, so I said:
>
> **"Coffee after my painting class at the Art Institute Wednesday?"**
>
> **"I'd rather watch you paint."**

I gladly told him where he'd find me in the upstairs Impressionist Gallery.

Eager to make a good first impression, I dressed in a cashmere v-neck over sleek French jeans. With my canvas set up about a foot from the original, I added final touches to my copy of Impressionist master, Pierre-Auguste Renoir's TWO SISTERS.

As I painted a rosy glow on my young girl's cheeks, I sensed watchful eyes behind me. Turning around, I expected to see JOURNEYMAN.

Instead, I saw twenty hushed students in navy plaid school uniforms, watching every stroke.

"I thought all artists were dead," said a young pudge ball with chocolate eyes.

I had to laugh, since I'd never felt more alive. "These artists lived a hundred years ago, but the beauty they created lives forever," I said.

A grinning boy with missing front teeth leapt toward me. "I want to be an artist."

I patted his bony shoulder and smiled. I could be the only copyist who didn't wear headphones to prevent these interruptions, because I loved to share a teachable tidbit now and then: "A Spanish artist named Picasso said we're all born artists," I said. "The secret is to keep our artist alive. Any ideas how we do that?"

A boy wearing thick glasses said, "Eat and sleep right."

"She means draw something," a girl told him.

"Whenever you do something you love, you're the artist of your own life," I said.

Their two chaperones waved thanks and herded the students into the next gallery. That's when I heard solo applause and saw the face I'd grown to love on my computer screen.

"Well said, SONGBIRD."

"JOURNEYMAN." I saw some delightful mischief in his eyes, and I wanted to hug him. He extended his hand, so I shook it with both of mine. "Great to see you in the flesh."

"So you didn't see me that night?" he asked.

"What night?" Coincidentally, my cell rang. It was Sharon, so I picked up. "Can't talk. Call you later."

Sharon shrieked, "Scottie just dumped me. Don't you dare go out with him."

Whoa. I don't do commands. My mind's eye flashed to Sharon sitting on the lap of her silver-haired *Mr. Lust,* and then I looked at my silver-haired JOURNEYMAN. *Damn.* I told her I'd stop by on my way home. I turned to him and watched for his reaction. "That was Sharon."

He shifted his weight and said, "That's what I came here to tell you."

"What?"

Scanning the wall of paintings, he said, "We weren't going to ride into the sunset together. We left on good terms. But there'd be hard feelings if you and I dated now."

"What are you saying? You dumped my friend?" I stammered. "And now you want to date me?"

"Not exactly," he said.

"You don't want to date me?" I asked.

"I do," he said. "That caused trouble when I told Sharon during lunch."

I looked away. *What else can I say to her Mr. Lust?*

"Should we wait a while? Before we go out?" he asked.

The prompt museum guard interrupted us to say it was time for me to pack up. I knelt on my blue tarp and JOURNEYMAN knelt on one knee, unconcerned about his business suit, and helped me load tubes of paint into my wooden caddy. When his shoulder brushed against mine, we looked at each other, silently acknowledging the energy sizzling between us.

Forget Sharon. He's for me, my wild woman thought. That's why I had to tame her. Mountain Men may come and go, but my tribe is forever.

We stood up, and I secured my tarp on my caddy. "You didn't answer my question," he said. As I put a finger on my cheek, playfully trying to remember his question, he said, "Let's talk about this over a drink."

"A drink?" We were walking out of my gallery as I said, "Then one day, I'd dive into your arms, and you'd dump me for someone new, like you dumped my friend." *Whoa. Lighten up.*

He stopped mid-stride. "Is that how you see me?"

"I heard it's your track record," I said. "Shall we take the high road?"

With a reluctant shrug, he seemed absorbed in his thoughts as we took the revolving door outside. Offering me his business card, he said, "Is it okay if we stay in touch?"

My feelings were brewing and I found words for them, "If not, I'd be disappointed." As I took his card, I got some purple paint on his hands.

While wiping them with a tissue, heat rushed into my cheeks. He must've noticed.

"Could be trouble," he said.

My wild woman liked the sound of it, as we walked away in opposite directions. Wanting one more glimpse of him for the road, I looked back as he glanced at me. *It's hard to let a good BAM go*, I chuckled to myself.

Pulling out of the Millennium Parking Lot, I drove north to Lincoln Park and met Sharon at Sweet Temptations, where everyone knew their neighbors. She was focused on a pastry and a chat with Max who greeted me with a supportive hug. Sharon's was tense.

Pointing for me to sit by Max, Sharon gave a command, "Stay away from Scottie."

I bristled and she lowered her voice. "He's a good pioneer, but a bad settler, like most guys who've been divorced less than a year."

"A good pioneer?" I asked.

"A pleasure pioneer," Sharon said. "Always after greener trails."

"Tails," Max said.

"You shouldn't date any guy during his first year," Sharon said, sipping her latte.

"Then why'd you date him right after his divorce?" I asked.

"That's when a pioneer's starved for fun. It's fun to be his feast," Sharon said. "But his tastes change like the wind, so beware. He'll run from a settler like you—until settling down looks good again, after a couple years of being free again."

Hmm. She might be onto something... "If Walter turned into a Pioneer when he left me, what made him turn back into a Settler?"

Max spoke up first. "Meeting someone he didn't want to lose." Watching us gasp, Max said, "An inconvenient truth of dating."

Sharon sighed, "Scottie's hardest to lose."

Her feelings for him made me dismiss mine. "Give it some time. See if he comes back to you," I said.

"Thanks. For not going out with him," Sharon said.

"How long do you have dibs on him?" I asked. *Not my finest moment.*

Max said, "It's a big pond so keep fishing. I wish I could. Mark finally did rehab after I nagged him into it. But now he's a dry drunk."

It's a day for new terms. "What's that?" I asked.

"When he's sober, he has to face all the crap he drowned with Jack," Max said. "And he's no fun. He's as prickly as one of your cactuses. Cacti?"

"Had I known this little secret earlier, I could've helped some people I loved," I said. "Mark needs a nutritional rescue, like everyone in recovery." *Will she be open to it?*

"I need a rescue," Max said. "I have to deal with all his issues, while you two can date and ditch as many guys as you want."

Sharon's tone softened, "I'd deal with some issues if it's part of our life saga, instead of another short story," she said. "I know this is politically incorrect, but I'm starting to think we won't get what we want."

Reluctantly, I nodded. Max said, "You don't know how good you've got it."

Dating. It's drained my enthusiasm—again. Time to change focus, Hadley girl.

That night I took a new look at my novel-in-progress and started writing "Chapter 2. ADVENTURER WANTED." In order to sculpt fiction from my real-life experiences, I had to recall the cheerful optimism I felt when I first envisioned my ideal mountain man. That way of thinking gradually revived my cheerful optimism. That's when I was ready to take action.

> For the first time in two weeks, I clicked on the dating site, eager to see if any hunters had contacted me. One tickled my fancy the old fashioned way—via email:

> **"Dear SONGBIRD, I'm SEEKER007, an American living in the mountains of Malaysia, developing land over here. I'm still a Midwestern boy at heart, who cares and loves deeply. My parents are happily married 52 years in a small town not far from yours. I want to love the way they do.**

> **"I'm seeking a sweet, strong, sexually and financially secure woman with Midwestern values, who understands**

the career demands of a world-class businessman and the emotional concerns of a single father. When I saw you and heard your voice, I wanted to give love again, not just receive it. If you like my profile, we should meet. Are you ready to be swept off your feet?"

Come to me, baby. Let's fall in love. I saw no reason not to trust my instincts, so we got to know each other through nightly phone conversations—since SEEKER007 said he didn't have quality video conferencing in his remote area.

Two weeks later, we made a big decision by phone. I was excited to share my news with my children, but I waited until I had both of them together—a captive audience at our Santa Fe Ski Basin on Easter weekend.

My skis shifted back and forth on our triple chairlift, and I lifted my goggles for a clear view of their reactions. "I'm taking a big step," I said. "I hope you support it."

Logan's snowboard dripped melting snow as we glided toward the powdery peak. "You're going half-way around the world to meet a guy named SPITBALL?"

"Speedball—nick-named for his Porsche racing," I said.

Logan shook his head. "Does he speak English?"

"Yes. He's an American developing land over there," I said. "We've talked on the phone every day for two weeks and I like what I've heard so far."

Jade lifted her goggles and asked the most important question from her teenage perspective. "What does he look like?"

A feisty stallion. I told them, "He's a little younger, tall, athletic and handsome. I'll show you his picture on the computer when we get home."

Jade leaned across her brother and poked me. "He really said *Mountains?*"

I patted her mittens. "In his first e-mail and several times after that. He thinks the mountain gods led us to each other."

Wiping his nose on his glove, Logan asked, "Will he cheat on you like Dad did?"

"You can stop blaming your dad for our breakup. I made mistakes, too."

Jade mumbled, "You didn't leave him for a young guy."

"Tina wasn't the reason we broke up. You can let that go, like I have."

"Then what was the reason?" Logan asked.

The moment I'd feared and imagined finally had arrived. They're old enough to see how their dad's work takes him away so much of the year. Could they see how an early lonely spell made me take a break from our marriage to feel less lonely? How I quickly realized I'd rather have rare but wonderful times with my husband than a life without him? How I'd told him that and he'd never mentioned it again, until he filed his divorce papers 23 years later? How I'd set the karma in motion for the breakup of our family?

I looked in their expectant eyes and felt I'd be unloading the weight I'd carried onto them. That wouldn't be fair.

"Your dad and I each felt overlooked at times. We hurt each other, but I thought we made up for it by being loving partners and parents."

"We thought you were happy," Jade said. "Dad said he loved you every time he saw you."

I'd been concerned they wouldn't trust his expressions of love, so I had to handle this carefully. "We felt a love that could've lasted forever, if—"

"If what?" Logan pressed me.

"If we could have stayed so focused on each other that we felt close even when we were far apart."

"So distance causes divorce?" Logan asked.

Adults spend a lifetime trying to figure this out. How do I help him? "It's more like, *what you lose focus on, you lose.*"

"Or what you focus on, you win," Logan said. He'd already made had a habit of flipping the switch.

I gave him a proud smile. "So we keep our eyes on love."

As our triple chair approached the unloading dock at the mountain peak, Jade scooted forward. "Could you love Speedball, Mom?"

"I could, or I wouldn't be traveling so far to meet him," I said.

We glided down the snow-packed ramp, and Jade challenged Logan to a race. He looked at me, and I said, " Go for it." *Ahhh. They're leaving me in their powder, as it should be.*

I enjoyed a gentle pace during that and other solo runs down the mountain that afternoon. Followed by dinner with the tribe in town, where Sarah and my kids reunited like long-lost sibs.

During my Good-Friday check up, I asked for a green light for my globetrotting from Doctor G.

He said, "New experiences grow new brain cells. If we're not growing, we're dying. So there's a health incentive for you to go."

That was the nudge I needed to make the trip.

Since Doctor G was part of our tribe, I invited him to join us for an Easter buffet at my club. That's when I met his new girlfriend, Lauren, a lanky Jungian therapist who'd been married to Nonnie's son for 10 years before their recent divorce. I was a bit envious to see Doctor G beaming at her. *Will SEEKER007 be that happy with me?*

The next week, Walter surprised me with his reaction to my upcoming trip. Arriving a few minutes early for his weekly dinner with Jade, he walked in the foyer while her band was practicing downstairs.

"The whole house is shaking. No wonder the dog is deaf," he said.

I hoisted Lily's hind legs with a rolled towel so she could walk over to him. Patting her head with his fingertips, as if afraid to get dog hairs on his Zegna suit, he said, "You shouldn't leave the country with the dog in such bad shape."

"Her new vet offered to take good care of her for twenty bucks a day."

"Logan called to say it might not be safe to travel to Malaysia right now."

I should've known my children would care as much for my well being as I do for theirs. "I heard it's the one spot where people of all religions get along."

"You can't afford that extravagant trip on what you earn as a sub."

Hmm. The better I look, the worse he behaves. "I'm using your divorce miles. Over there, a five-star hotel's cheaper than a Holiday Inn over here."

"I'd like your itinerary," he said.

"So you can track my adventures?" I teased.

He gave me that grin that showed his dimples. "In case of emergency. Who's the lucky guy?"

"Jealous?" As Walter gave me a penetrating gaze with his dark eyes, I saw his pupils dilate into big saucers, clearly aroused. *Whoa. Me, too. Now what?* I wondered as we held each other in our gaze. Wisely, we looked away, acting as if nothing had happened.

At six in the morning of my departure day, I went back to the gym for some pre-flight exercise and to drum up support from my tribe of spinners.

Dolly was a tough sell. "You must be desperate, going so far to meet a man."

I checked my pulse monitor and sped up to get into my fat-burning zone. "It's an adventure," I said. "Rocket fuel for my writing."

Meeka nodded. "It might be time to expand her horizons."

"You could travel a million miles and stay stuck in the friendship rut," Dolly said, while dousing her forehead with bottled water.

"I hope not," I said.

After spinning, my exfoliated body was robotically sprayed with a mystic tan to launch my ten thousand mile journey to meet my *Mountain Man.*

SEEKER007 (Paul Martin) had told me, after I'd explained Sharon's latest dating theory, that his Pioneer years were over and he was ready to be a Settler again.

"Then I'm optimistic about our meeting," I'd said.

It wasn't until I boarded my flight that I felt my first tremor of fear. I had no idea what would be waiting for me in that tropical paradise.

6. MEETING CHALLENGES

After two long days on planes from Chicago to Kuala Lumpur, interrupted by a quick nap in a windowless bunk in Singapore airport, I felt as if I were still flying during my limo ride from the Kuala Lumpur airport to the Mandarin Oriental Hotel. Since Paul Martin's limo driver made no effort to chat, I sat back and enjoyed the lush tropical scenery.

Fifteen minutes into our drive, I saw a military caravan heading in the opposite direction. "What's with all those tanks?" I asked, but my driver didn't respond. *Does he know English? I should've learned some phrases in whatever language they speak over here.*

The driver handed me a cell phone and a box of chocolates. "Mr. Martin wants you to call him. I wrote his number on my card."

"So you speak English, and very well," I said.

"It's the language of world power, so we must use it."

As requested, I phoned Paul Martin. He said he was in a meeting and he'd meet me later at my hotel. Click. *Oh well.* I glanced out the open window.

"I didn't expect to be driving on the left."

"Leftover from past British rule," the driver said.

I noticed beads of sweat forming where his dark hair almost touched the rim of his Nehru collar. "I like your five-day holiday," I said. "We have three-day holidays in the U.S."

He glanced back at me, "It is a Muslim holy weekend, honoring the birthday and teachings of Prophet Muhammed. Our Malidur Rasul celebration."

I repeated the phrase and propped myself against the back of his leather seat. "How do you celebrate?"

While passing two VW sedans, he said, "With Quran recitals and speeches calling on Muslims to better ourselves with more knowledge, more unity with non-Muslims, and to embody the values of Muhammed each day."

"If we were kind to people and our planet, we'd embody the values of every great prophet, wouldn't we?" I asked rhetorically.

He didn't respond. I saw another caravan of tanks approaching us. "Is there a military parade this weekend?"

Instead of a reply, he used his speed dial and had a hushed cell chat. I tried to believe it was nothing.

An hour later, he drove up to the entrance of famed Petranoss towers beside my hotel. A doorman dressed like a Buckingham Palace guard removed my tweed carry-on bag from the trunk. As another royal guard helped me out of the limo, I realized, *They make me feel like a visiting queen.* I waved to my driver, but he sped away without noticing.

My two-room suite also was fit for a queen. I headed into the shower and enjoyed its simulated wildlife calls and rain forest waterfalls, which I planned to see for real on this trip. I dressed quickly for my dinner date with Paul, but there was no need to rush.

In a two-hour lull without word from him, I kept busy. I set out a recent family photo with my kids at Nonnie's house for dinner, which I brought along to show Paul. I wrote hotel postcards and mailed them through the concierge in the lobby.

I returned to my room and sampled local TV news, like I usually did in a new country. That's when I began to piece together clues about a local rebellion.

I watched a Thai religious leader hold up the Quran and shout in English, "Thai soldiers slaughtered our young boys against the laws of Islam, which forbid Muslims from attacking churches or temples, even in times of war."

A man identified as a Thai separatist promised more attacks and warned tourists to stay away from Thai resorts in the South during weekend celebrations.

I grabbed the tourist guidebook on my Queen Anne desk and checked how close KL was to Southern Thailand. *Too close for comfort.* I paid close attention to the following interview:

Malaysian Prime Minister Abdullah announced he sent tanks to patrol border towns to prevent Thai insurgents from seeking refuge here. He said that it was difficult to turn away border residents who commute regularly to work in KL. He had considered providing temporary refuge for Thai nationals who wanted to escape the latest clashes. He concluded, "We don't know what's going to happen this weekend, so it's best for Malays to stay at home."

Now that I understood the mission for that parade of tanks, I wondered, *What am I doing here?* That's when my new cell phone rang, and Paul Martin said in his deep, comforting voice, "Come down to the lobby. I can't wait to meet you."

I walked into the bustling lobby, ready to leap into the arms of a tall American with dark hair, sleek build and impeccable grooming. Standing two heads above the local crowd, I saw a tall American with grey hair, beefy build and sloppy grooming, with his shirt sleeves rolled up to his elbows.

"Paul?" I asked, trying to hide my disappointment. When he nodded and smiled, I couldn't fake a smile. I'd fallen for an old portrait of the man he used to be—maybe ten years and twenty pounds ago.

Instead of giving him the big kiss I'd hoped for, I shook his clammy hand and watched sweat roll down his neck and soak his oxford shirt. *NEXT! Get back on the dating site!* That's what I decided at first glance.

As we walked into the hotel restaurant, I was immersed in my thoughts: *Thankfully, I'd been honest with him. I'd warned him that I saw most dates as platonic friends. He'd promised to change that, but that'll never happen with him. Thankfully, I paid my own way here. He has no grounds to feel I owe him anything but friendship. Even that debt's questionable. If I dumped him now, I'd be marooned here. Hmm. I liked his company on the phone, so why not make the best of it? Unless—*

"You're awful quiet," Paul said, as we sat down at a corner table.

"I'm hungry," I said, noticing the flattering effect of candlelight on his tanned face.

He signaled for the waiter and we ordered Australian lamb for me, and Chateaubriand for two (just for him), with a bottle of his favorite

Australian red. When I expressed my concern over the violence in Southern Thailand, Paul said he'd take his sons and leave if they weren't totally safe here. I breathed a sigh of relief.

Throughout our two-hour meal, we traded pictures and stories about our children.

"I'm glad all four of our kids are on the fast track," he said. "That's important for my next marriage."

Why burst his bubble during dinner?

When the check came and he didn't reach for it, I signed it to my room. Then Paul tried to close our deal like the *world-class businessman* he'd said he was. "Friend or more? What's it going to be?"

"Let's spend some time together as friends, and see what happens."

He touched my hand. "I've got enough friends. I want to love you."

I tucked our dinner receipt in my wallet and stood up. Instead of rising like a gentleman, he leaned back in his chair. "What's your verdict?"

This is what he gets for forcing the issue. "It's *Friends*," I said. "I can't tell if that'll change, since I barely slept since I left home."

As Paul followed me out of the restaurant, he sounded annoyed, "I'm in the middle of a big deal, so I can't waste my time if this isn't going anywhere."

Reaching the brass bank of elevators, I faced him. "I'm still up for the activities we talked about. But I'm happy to explore on my own, if you're not interested."

The elevator opened and he seemed reluctant to let me walk inside. "Let's play tennis early tomorrow, before it gets hot," he said.

"See you in the morning," I said, as the elevator doors wiped him from view. I practically sleepwalked to my room. Without undressing, I dove into a mound of pillows. As I was drifting off, I remembered a promise I'd made.

I phoned Jade and left her this voicemail: "Hi Sweetie. I met Paul Martin. He'll never be more than a friend, and all is well. Love you."

For the next twelve hours I slept so soundly that I didn't hear the phone ring when Paul had tried to reach me twice that morning.

Luckily, I felt like a new person when we played tennis on the secluded hotel courts in the mid-day sun. While I was beating Paul at his *2nd favorite game after golf*, I was on the lookout for the slightest reason to cross the boundary I'd set at friendship.

Possibly due to the intense heat, Paul's personality quirks surfaced when I smashed another nice point. He shouted a profanity loud enough for people in the pool to hear, and he slammed a tennis ball over the ivy wall onto the street below us.

"You have a temper," I said. He grinned like a boy caught in a cookie jar.

"You ain't no better than me," he said.

I did a double take. "That's no way to talk to a grammar teacher."

He nodded, as if reminding himself to speak correctly near me.

When our match was tied, I suggested we end it. He agreed.

We walked into the café outside Petranoss towers. Paul asked for *a double cup* three times, and the server behind the counter ignored him. I whispered, "Say, Please." He did, and instantly received the double he desired.

As we looked for an empty table, I noticed most women were covered up in cloth from head to toe. I asked, "Is it disrespectful to wear a tennis dress in public?

Sipping his espresso, he said, "They're very tolerant of our ways here. The Middle East is a different story."

When Paul left to do some business in town, I swam laps for ten minutes and then took a nap. Around seven, Paul picked me up for golf on a course that was lighted for night play. His 12 and 15-year old sons, Andrew and Keith, played with us. They were polite and friendly. *He raised great kids on his own. Don't write him off so fast, Hadley girl.*

Unfortunately, more of his quirks surfaced when he handed me a crappy set of clubs, no driver or woods, and expected me to lug the bag on my shoulder. When he lied to the golf starter, in front of his two sons, by saying I was listed on his club membership so he could save a few bucks on guest fees, I balked. I quietly paid my guest fee, rented clubs and hired a local caddy, all for $45.

Before we teed off, the golf starter politely asked Paul's two sons to tuck their shirts into their pants. Instantly, the boys did so, as Paul whispered to me, "That guy hates Americans, like most people around here. Since I do business here, I'm learning to laugh it off."

At the fourth hole, I laughed it off when Paul's long drive landed by some tall trees and his ball was surrounded by a gang of white-faced monkeys. They allowed me, my caddy and Paul's two sons to pass by, but they closed ranks when Paul approached and refused him access to his second shot. *What are they telling me about him?*

"Is that how you treat rich Americans?" Paul shouted at the gang during their face-off.

A defiant monkey held up Paul's golf ball like a trophy and launched peels of laughter in everyone but Paul. As he walked away with a size-able chip on his shoulder instead of his golf ball, I thought, *The monkeys won that hole.*

Throughout the round, I noticed Paul often praised the golf skills of his older son, Keith, which may have caused his younger son, Andrew, to pick up his ball on the toughest hole, apparently giving up trying to be as good as his brother.

I walked over to the discouraged son and patted his shoulder. "I'm amazed how well you play for a boy who's only been on this earth for twelve years."

Andrew smiled and kept playing. He started hitting all his shots near mine, showing great skill, so we could walk and talk together for the rest of the round. Paul often trailed behind us, smiling when I looked back at him.

When we played a swampy hole, a platoon of mosquitoes singled me out for attack and I ran while swatting my whole body.

"You're so sweet, they love you," Paul said. "But you should've worn repellent, or you could catch Dengue Fever. My friend was deathly ill from it for months."

"You should've warned me," I said. *Is my immune system stronger than Dengue Fever?*

After we finished nine holes, I ate a burger at the clubhouse with *the three boys*. I'd demoted Paul, who seemed less mature than his two sons.

As he drove me back to my hotel in his Porsche convertible, I saw how he earned the name Speedball. "I wish I had a brake on my side," I said. He nodded and slowed down.

"It's sweet of you to drive me all this way, Paul."

"Because I care. If I didn't you'd be in a taxi."

Ouch. Returning to the hotel, I watched his behavior change. A gentleman emerged from his Porsche. Paul opened my door and walked me into the lobby.

"I'm ready to go full speed ahead," he said. "You're too cute, now that you look like your pictures."

"When I'm tired and windblown?"

"When your defenses are down, I see the girl I'd like to know."

I gave him a peck on the cheek. He held my arm, so I couldn't walk away. "I'm heading to the beach with my boys for a couple days. Are you in or out?"

"In. If I have my own room."

With downcast eyes, he said, "At least you're honest."

"We both wanted us to click right away, but it didn't happen," I said. "Though I'd still like to explore the rainforest with you."

"That's too much driving. Not relaxing for me."

"I'll hire a driver. My treat."

Backing away, he said, "Why don't you do that while I'm on the Islands. I'll call you in a couple days."

Watching Paul walk out of the hotel, I thought, *I'm on my own. Again.* Thankfully, I didn't feel so alone when I snuggled into my mound of pillows and stroked my cheek the way Walter used to, before I drifted to sleep.

Sunrise brightened my prospects for Plan B. Looking out my window to the park by the hotel, I saw a couple dozen locals doing Tai Chi. I'd tried that a few times at my gym, so I jumped into my lilac yoga outfit and joined the group's gentle, 88-move routine, which could be revved up if needed for self defense. *Even without a leader, everyone knows the drill.*

Afterwards, the locals quietly went on their peaceful ways and the only other westerner in the group walked up to me. "Are you staying at the hotel?" she asked.

I invited the friendly woman in Nike sweats to join me for breakfast. She was married to an ambassador, and English was her third language. When I told her why I came to KL, she said she knew *The Big American* from workouts in the hotel spa.

While listening to her recommendations for day-tours to book through the hotel, I glanced at the grandfatherly man at the next table who was reading a newspaper headline: AMERICA HAS NEVER BEEN MORE HATED.

"What happened?" I asked, but he didn't look up.

"American abuse of Iraqi prisoners, I'm afraid," the ambassador's wife told me. "I'm late for a meeting. Will I see you in the park Tuesday morning?"

"I'll look forward to it," I said, signing our breakfast bill to my room.

We hugged good-bye like fast friends. Then I walked over to the concierge and asked to book a guided tour to the rainforest. In a rude tone, he told me there were no openings until Thursday, and then he looked around me to the next person in line.

"Excuse me. Could I rent a car and driver?" I asked.

Now he sounded annoyed. "All fully booked all weekend. Next!"

That rejection was all too familiar. I walked away, intending to check out the hotel spa. A rail-thin teenage boy stepped in front of me. "Do you want a driver, Miss?"

"Are you old enough to drive?"

He stood up straighter. "My client cancelled, so I take you on a tour."

"Of the rainforest?"

Nodding again, he said, "Five hundred ringgetts. Cash."

Only 150 bucks for a private tour? "Do you have references?"

"Hotel guests. Or I would not be in here."

"Deal." I rummaged through my fanny pack for his fare and gave it to him.

He counted it and bowed. "I am Thanksin Shinawatra. Your guide."

"Hadley Finch. Thanks for working on a holiday." As I followed him to the livery sign, I saw his smile grow into an amused sigh. "What's so funny?"

"Thanksin Shinawatra is our Prime Minister. You Americans know nothing of our country." He walked up to his motorbike and handed me a scuffed helmet. I gave it right back. "You don't want a tour?" he asked with a sly grin.

I glanced at his mini motorbike. "Can it carry two of us?"

"Have you looked around?"

I saw no need to do so. "Any other options?"

He shrugged. "We drive your car. You walk. Or stay here until drivers go back to work."

I'd traveled this far for adventure, but I questioned whether I should place my fate in the hands of this young kid. "I'm not up for a bike ride. Sorry," I said.

Without my having to ask, he returned my fare. While walking away, I saw the royal guards shoo him away from the livery station and then he sped off on his scooter. *Hmm...* I headed for the hotel spa.

Apparently, nobody used the spa on a holiday weekend, so a 20ish male trainer was available to guide my workout on the weight machines, followed by stretching on the mat. I yelled, *STOP*, when he pressed my extended leg too far and it hurt my back.

"Must work on flexibility," he said.

I'd been bending instead of breaking lately. But my body's not as flexible as my spirit. Time for yoga, Hadley girl, I thought, while walking into the restroom.

While taking my seat on the throne, I got a whiff of harsh cleaning chemicals the attendant was using in the next stall. I sneezed three times, in rapid fire, and shrieked as my back froze. *Yikes. I'm stuck on the john.*

I breathed through the tension until it eased up. Holding onto the toilet paper stand, I pulled myself up and relieved most of the pressure in my back. For the first time, I faced a new likelihood—*Today's fifty might not be yesterday's thirty after all.*

As the cleaning attendant watched me shuffle past her, she said, "Need a doctor?"

"A masseuse," I said.

Fifteen minutes later, I was lying face down on a massage table, welcoming the relief of the essential oils and gentle fingertips of the therapist. Neither one of us said a word until the end of the hour, when she asked if I felt better.

"Would you work on the tense spot here, please," I said, pointing to my back.

The instant she used stronger pressure, I felt jolts of electricity shoot up my spine. With each jolt, I shrieked. She excused herself to call a doctor, leaving me there in sizzling pain. *I wouldn't be here if Walter didn't leave me. Damn him.*

Rushing back to me, she said, "The doctor is an hour away. Will your husband take you to the hospital?"

"I'm alone," I sighed. Luckily, I was lying face down so she couldn't see my unavoidable tears.

She told me a change of position would help. When she helped me rotate onto my back, another blast of shooting pain made me freeze like a statue in her arms. Her support was the only thing that stopped the sizzling, so she held me like that while we waited over an hour for the doctor.

Since she weighed a hundred pounds at most, this exercise had to sap her strength. I kept thanking her for holding me up—until she spoke up.

"It's my job to help people. Even Americans," she said. "I'm used to a hard life."

"How so?" I asked, hoping her story would distract me from mine.

Each time she spoke, I felt her warm breath on my back as she described her life on a farm in Southern Thailand, an hour away by motorbike. She told me they had no electricity, no plumbing. They washed clothes in a stream. Plowed land by hand. Raised chickens for eggs, and on special days for its flesh. They went to sleep when it got dark. There were no single men nearby to marry.

"Will you move to the city someday?" I asked.

"I'm the only support for my mother. My sisters. My life is there," she said.

When the doctor finally arrived twenty minutes later than estimated, he couldn't move me out of her arms without causing radiating pain. So he asked her to hold me up while he injected my right hip with liquid fire and gave me pain pills with water. He left before they kicked in.

When a half hour passed without any relief, I said, "I need another shot."

She giggled, "You'd be ready to party."

I almost wished I'd chosen that option. I don't remember much of what happened once those meds kicked in. For the next few days, I'd open my eyes from woozy sleep and meals would be set up on a bedside tray, as if appearing by magic.

Once I caught a groggy glimpse of a TV news story about the champion soccer team, shot and killed in a mosque by Thai police:

"The terrorists bought guns to fight for a Muslim separate state," said the police chief.

"The boys wouldn't care about that if they had jobs after soccer," a father said.

"They never hurt anyone. They were good boys," said a grieving mother.

"Good with machetes. They beheaded a Thai policemen near the mosque," said the police chief.

"My son ran off. He told me the Indos came to practice and insisted they fight as hard for a separate state as they did to win the championship title. Now he is forbidden to show his face here," a father said.

"Three boys ran off, leaving their teammates to face their maker. Thai justice will be quick. Those boys will be shot on sight," said the police chief.

In my half-conscious state, I trembled because of one sound byte. If those boys wouldn't care about a terrorist fight if they had jobs to do after soccer, wasn't that a path to peace? I knew Einstein had said, *If the solution's simple, it's God talking.* But who's listening when God speaks through parents of *terrorists?* I conked out in frustration.

I started coming back to life the next day, as I heard the hotel manager knock before entering my room. He seemed surprised to find me awake. "Will you check out as planned?"

I sat up in bed without much pain. "Yes, I will. Thanks for the flowers and room service."

"The least we could do." Before he left, he gave me a message from Paul Martin. I never opened it.

I pulled myself out of bed and took a shower in my simulated rain forest waterfall—that was the closest I got to the real thing during my tropical adventure.

7. ALTERNATIVES

As I hobbled into my nest, Jade gasped, "You walk like an old lady."

"I'm walking," I said, reaching out for her gentle hug. Breathing in the floral scent of her hair, still damp from her shower, filled me with so much joy. "I'm so glad to see you," I sighed.

"In time for carry-out."

"Simple pleasures," I said. *Uh-huh. Each pleasure is simply profound.*

Jade had set out containers of food in the dining room and arranged for Logan to join us for dinner by speaker-phone as soon as we sat down. I launched our conversation with an embarrassing admission, "A sneeze hurt my back after too much exercise, so I spent most of my trip resting in my room."

"What was wrong with Speedball?" Jade asked, between bites.

"A big chip on his shoulder. Plus he looked much older than his picture—an honesty issue, because he was still handsome. I didn't see him after my back injury."

Logan said, "Sammy Sosa blew out his back with a sneeze before a Cubs game the same day you did. That's how I'll remember your trip."

He signed off, and Jade told me about her band's first paid show that I missed at a teen club in Chicago. I promised to be at her next show.

That night, when my pain pills made me violently ill, I wondered—*Did this also happen to Sammy Sosa?*

Pain teaches me to ask for help, I thought as I walked into the Georgian home of our neighborhood orthopedic surgeons, Doctors Kabir and Meeka.

I handed them my MRI's, which I'd posed for the day before. Holding them up to the light, Kabir pointed out three dark lines where three plump white discs were meant to be.

I said the first thing that came to mind, "Inject them."

"No one does that, or we would've read studies," Kabir said.

Meeka gave me a prognosis. "You don't need surgery. You do need steroids, safer pain pills and a few months of serious rest."

Glancing outside at their backyard swimming pool, I realized that meant a summer without the sporting life I'd longed for all winter. I left there, thinking—*There has to be another way in Santa Fe. When will I feel up to flying again?*

I celebrated Mothers Day during my first weekend home, while I sat on my garden chaise and watched Jade and Logan, now home for summer vacation, plant hibiscus bushes to create our own tropical garden.

"To go so far, when the beauty was right here," I said.

"That's what great odysseys are about," Logan said, while watering his plantings.

"How do you know?" Jade challenged him.

"I just aced the final." Logan sprayed Jade with the hose, and they regressed into a tug of war for its control. I knew I'd get sprayed, and I delighted in a splash of the good old days.

When Lily jumped into the fray, her hind legs collapsed. Logan helped her up. "Her jumping days are over," he said.

When I'd thought mine were too, I came up with a new plan that definitely got their attention when I announced it: "It's time to start *Home Care Boot Camp* so you know how to take care of yourselves when I'm not around." They looked so shocked, I had to laugh. "It's Mother's Day. Humor me."

Lily benefited from their first lesson—how to give her a tub bath with a blow dry and a bow. Next stop was the kitchen. "We've got to cook dinner?" Jade whined.

"It's not cooking dinner. It's nourishing loved ones," I said, showing them my new favorite cookbook, *Dining In The Raw*.

Jade poked her brother, "You've got to eat naked." He swatted her arm, which knocked a measuring cup filled with lentils onto the floor. A perfect segue into my vacuuming lesson.

I gave Logan the electric broom, "This is the Zamboni. And this is the rink," I said, pointing to the floor. "Clean the ice, Tiger."

Logan reminded me of his dad when he'd used our mighty Hoover in our tiny apartment and together we'd clean our whole place in an hour. *Before a big house and a live-in housekeeper. It's back to the simple life again. I need everyone to pitch in.*

While I was showing them how to cook up Plan B—minestrone, Walter made his traditional Mother's Day call: "Thanks for giving me two great kids, and for all you did to make them that way."

"I enjoyed their childhoods as much as they did," I said.

"You did something right, Dalai Momma."

"Dalai Momma?" I almost giggled as I repeated that new term.

Logan pointed to his sister, as if it were her idea. Jade gave me a soft squeeze, and I said, "It doesn't get any better than this." A few hours later it did.

During my bubble bath, JOURNEYMAN called me. "*Happy Mother's Day*, Hadley. Are you as devoted to your man as you are to your kids?"

"I'd like to be," I said.

I must've splashed, because he asked, "Are you in the tub—naked?"

"I am. And there's room for two."

"Ooohh. I'll be back in town later this week."

I remembered why I couldn't see him. "What about Sharon?"

"It's been a month with no urge to get back with her. I'm a free agent."

"She called you a pioneer, always after greener trails. Sorry I said that."

"You know her strategy. What kind of friend doesn't want you to be happy?"

"Let's give it more time," I said, smacking my bubbles in frustration.

A week later I tested my back—I couldn't lift a grocery bag but I could swim a few laps at our local pool. Then I received a test via video chat:

> **"Hey, SONGBIRD. How much time? We aren't getting any younger. Your man, JOURNEYMAN"**
>
> **"You're right. Let's talk after I go to Santa Fe to fix a minor back injury."**
>
> **"You shouldn't go through that alone, SONGBIRD. Want some company?"**
>
> *Absolutely. But what about Sharon? How long do I put her needs before mine?* I answered my own test question:
>
> **"You can stay in my guest house. I'm excited to spend some time with you."**

The timing of our arrival at the 1940's airport in Santa Fe could've been orchestrated by the mountain gods.

"After traveling a thousand miles from opposite directions, after both of our flights were delayed, after I drove an hour from Albuquerque Airport, your plane flies right over my car as we arrive here at the same instant."

That was my version of hello, when JOURNEYMAN climbed out of his white corporate jet and gave me a big hug on the tarmac.

"What a coincidence," he said.

"It's the mountain gods' way of remaining anonymous. My spin on Carl Jung."

"I can learn something dating a teacher," he said, while helping me into my SUV.

"If you keep an open mind," I said, smiling at the thought of dating him.

As I drove by the plaza in the heart of town, I pointed out the long portal (porch) where Native Americans from a few dozen pueblos sold handmade silver, turquoise and artifacts every day, except Christmas.

While passing the stately capital building, I said, "That's Governor Richardson's office, a few blocks away from Doctor G."

"Your back doctor?"

"He's also helped my heart since my breakup. A full-service body shop," I said. He looked skeptical.

As we walked into Doctor G's adobe office, a 40ish Native American with a long black braid, wearing blue jeans and Nikes, was paying his bill. Doctor G's office manager, a Spanish woman named Mercedes, introduced us to the chief of a nearby pueblo.

"Don't you have a medicine man?" JOURNEYMAN asked playfully.

The chief nodded. "Nobody has all the answers."

Doctor G walked out of his treatment room and kissed my hand. "Are you ready to be tortured?"

I forgot to warn JOURNEYMAN about his sense of humor. "I brought a witness," I said, introducing two significant men in my life. Then I gave my MRI's to Doctor G, who looked at them while we followed him into his treatment room.

I took my seat on a leather massage-style table as JOURNEYMAN sat in a spectator's chair upholstered with a red Navaho blanket.

Doctor G pointed to images of my three blown discs. "I'll inject them," he said.

"That was my instinct," I said. "My MD's said nobody does that."

"What they don't know can hurt you. So you'll show them another way," he said. "After a few rounds of shots, your back will be as good as new."

"What qualifies you to stick needles in her back?" JOURNEYMAN asked.

"Each state has different licensing. I've been doing this treatment for years," Doctor G said. Then he motioned for me to lie down on the table.

"First, some detective work," I told JOURNEYMAN who watched Doctor G do his muscle testing in silence. A few minutes later, Doctor G looked at the vials that weakened my raised arm, and announced his diagnosis:

"You're cute, but rusty," he said. "You've got an army of free radicals we need to disarm before those shots can work."

"How long will that take?" I asked.

"One molecular shift causes an instant shift in the entire biochemistry." Rubbing his hands together, Doctor G grinned, "You should be ready for harpooning tomorrow."

I could see why JOURNEYMAN shook his head, but I liked Doctor G's playful attitude. It told me he had the utmost confidence in his health-care abilities. He prescribed four doses of a dozen natural supplements (like vitamin C and E, alpha lipoic acid, biotin and magnesium) before I saw him again the next morning. I took the first dose before we left the office.

As we walked to my car, JOURNEYMAN asked, "Why trust muscle testing when machines give you precise readings for everything?"

"I've felt the results. I trust my feelings."

"I hope you know what you're doing."

Nodding, I invited him to lunch and learned he had a long conference call starting in 20 minutes.

"Come with me," I said. I cut a couple minutes off the drive to my home in the dusty hills outside of town. Then I gave JOURNEYMAN my guest casita for privacy during his call. It started the moment I opened the door to leave.

Hmm. That's what I used to do for Walter. I slipped into the same old rhythm, without missing a beat.

Since it was another sunny day in my land of enchantment, I headed up to my roof deck for a half hour of naked sunbathing—following Doctor G's daily program to replenish vitamin D. I must've dozed, because JOURNEYMAN's voice startled me.

"You're shimmering," he said.

"It's the almond oil." I reached for him in a way that said my wild woman was ready to play. Leaving his linen shirt and cotton slacks in a heap on the wooden slats, he slowly, respectfully tested to see if my back could support the

weight of our passion. It couldn't. So I guided him onto his back, and then I melted into his arms.

The next thing I noticed, the hot sun woke me by scorching my back. "Loving you is feeling the sun on both sides," I said.

"That's nice," he said, smiling like he felt the same way, while I lay in his arms.

As I read the scene I'd written in my journal while sunbathing naked on my roof deck, I had a major *Aha. I'd wandered into erotic fantasies—the way I did when I felt overlooked by Walter.*

Instead of complaining like I did with Walter, I decided to fulfill my new fantasy with JOURNEYMAN—after I satisfied my more pressing hunger for a good meal.

At the end of his three-hour phone call, JOURNEYMAN joined me on my portal (porch) with a Sangre Mountain view.

"I'm light headed," he said. "How 'bout an early dinner to make up for our lost afternoon?"

We dined at Santa Café in a garden blooming with possibilities. Southwestern flavors and snippets of our life stories sparked my desire, especially while he held my hand between courses. I promised him a magical ending to our evening and asked him to help me set the stage as soon as we got home.

"Your wish is my pleasure," he said.

We each carried an air mattress and Indian blanket up the winding stairway to my roof deck. Then we settled down and watched the *big-sky show*, while I snuggled in his arms. We cheered at the sight of three shoot-ing stars. I knew how they felt. *Why'd I have that third glass of red? Whoa.* Fade to black.

I woke with a start on my roof deck, seeing JOURNEYMAN asleep beside me. I noticed we were stuck in the same pose as when I'd left us. *Damn. What a disappointment I must've been. Do I wake him? He looks so content in dreamtime…Four years since my last sleepover and this is it? Oh, well. It's lovely. And chilly.*

I tucked us into the blankets and breathed out my next string of thoughts so I could join him in dreamtime. As I drifted off, I think he asked me to roll over.

Happily, the sun wasn't the only thing rising at dawn. Our energy had been revived in the mountain air. The moment I'd imagined since my first *BAM* at the Art Institute had arrived.

Our intimate connection began in our eyes. While we explored the landscape of our bodies, I thought, *I'll never get enough of him.* I must've been beaming when I said, "Thanks, Mountain Man."

"Who?"

"You're a gift from the mountain gods, or whatever energetic force sent you to me."

"You're a kook," he said, grinning. "And easy to be with."

"You like that?" I asked.

"I love that," he said.

A good sign.

I was Doctor G's first patient that morning. He was chipper, humming a tune from the 40's when we walked in. After assuming our usual positions in his treatment room, Doctor G muscle tested various vials of liquids on my belly and collected ones that strengthened me.

"You want lots of goodies to grow new discs," he said.

"Where are the studies that prove this stuff works?" JOURNEYMAN asked.

"They're walking without pain, all over this country and beyond," Doctor G said, while he slid on a pair of latex gloves.

JOURNEYMAN's inquisition didn't seem to bother Doctor G, but it was stressing me. So I asked him to either be a silent witness or go read a magazine in the waiting room. He promised to be quiet.

When I heard Doctor G draw liquids into a syringe, I laid face down on the table so I wouldn't see the needle.

"That's one hell of a needle," JOURNEYMAN said.

"Uh," I shouted. Again he promised to be quiet.

I felt Doctor G swab my back and poke his gloved finger into a hot spot in my disc. He asked Scott to hold my hand for moral support. Then he asked me to take a deep breath and exhale slowly while he injected warm fluid near the *facet* of my disc.

"Oooh. You're jacking up my flat tire," I said, describing my sense of relief.

When we repeated that pattern the second time, I shrieked. Doctor G withdrew the needle and said my pain was his guide. I should feel localized pressure, not pain while he guided my breathing through his next injection.

During my next inhale, JOURNEYMAN slumped against me, and I shrieked again.

"He's not the first spectator to go down," Doctor G said. He asked Mercedes to revive Scott with smelling salts and help him into the waiting room.

Without further distractions and with minor discomfort, I breathed through seven more injections and did some gentle bicycle exercises to get the fluid flowing into my discs. The whole procedure took 30 minutes.

Afterwards, I walked with a lighter step into the waiting room, where JOURNEYMAN was holding his head in his hands.

"Not our best date," I said. "Luckily, he wasn't injecting you."

"I'd never go to a fringe doctor like him," he said, without looking up.

If he's against this, I can't be with him, I thought. *But I won't think NEXT until my full recovery gives him the proof that might change his mind.*

Doctor G walked up to Scott and asked to check wrist pulses before he let him leave. JOURNEYMAN offered both wrists and whined like a boy, "What if I'm too dizzy to golf today?"

Doctor G advised Scott to rest today and play golf tomorrow. He told me I should only putt on this trip.

"You think I'll be golfing this summer?" I asked.

"After your third round of shots, I'll join you for a round of golf," Doctor G said.

JOURNEYMAN perked up, "Count me in."

I felt giddy from all that good news when I charged my $978 bill for an *outpatient surgical procedure*. JOURNEYMAN glanced at my bill. "Is it covered by insurance?"

Doctor G beat me to a response, "By workmen's comp in my Arizona office. But most states don't know how to fix a flat this elegantly."

"Luckily, I can still afford it," I said, wishing I hadn't. That was an unintended segue into my current and future financial condition, which JOURNEYMAN asked me about while I drove us home. I told him my business plan to invest in my book and music so I could support myself when my divorce support dwindled down.

With a cocky smile he said, "I'd like to recommend safer investments. The fund I manage has outperformed the Dow by double digits for 15 years."

I still intended to fund my creative endeavors as I thanked him, thinking, *That's how he shows me he cares.*

That night I couldn't wait to introduce JOURNEYMAN to my tribe during dinner by an outdoor kiva (fireplace) at the club where Walter and I still shared our membership.

JOURNEYMAN was a good sport, agreeing to be the only guy to dine with *three generations of Santa Fe-bred blondes, who treated me like family*. That's how I introduced him to Nonnie, Karly and her daughter, Sarah, and he gave them each a quick hug.

When they introduced us to another guest of our tribe, a soft-spoken French woman named Solange, I noticed she held his hug a little longer and gave him a bigger smile.

She didn't take her eyes off him during dinner, while she dominated the conversation with reasons why she'd moved here from Paris to open a French bakery near the Plaza. When she and JOURNEYMAN had a lively conversation in French, excluding the rest of us from their banter, I cringed.

My loyal friend, Karly, drew JOURNEYMAN's focus away from that *Belle du Jour* and back where it belonged—on his date. "Did you hear about Hadley's hole-in-one?" she asked.

His jaw dropped. I explained, "My *mulligan* drowned and my next drive landed in the hole, so Walter said it was a hole-in-two plus a water penalty."

"If he allowed the mulligan, it's a hole in one," JOURNEYMAN said, sounding like my ally.

When Karly mentioned the short film I'd starred in, I took my cue. "During my breakup I played a jilted artist who clings to the dream of love," I said. "That dream inspired me to sign up for a SOULFULDATE. I've traveled to Malaysia to meet a match."

"Would you travel around the world with me, SONGBIRD?" he asked, in front of everyone. All eyes waited for my reply:

"I'd love to," I said. "When my nest is empty next year, I get my wings." His downcast eyes told me that might not be soon enough for him.

"There's one good thing about not having children," Solange said. "I'm free to do whatever, whenever I please."

JOURNEYMAN nodded like he got her green light, and I cringed again.

"Have you dated much since your divorce?" Solange asked.

"Mostly a friend of Hadley's," JOURNEYMAN said.

Damn. I forgot to mention it. They looked at me expectantly. "Sharon," I said. "She called him Mr. *Lust*, so I figured there was no future in it."

Mr. *Lust* nodded. Nonnie rolled her eyes. Karly shook her head. And her daughter, Sarah, asked, "What did Sharon say?"

JOURNEYMAN and I looked at each other and shrugged.

"You didn't tell her?" Nonnie shrieked.

"Isn't all fair in love and war?" Solange said.

"There's an honor code of dating," I said. "I'll talk to Sharon when I get home."

"Silly Americans," Solange said.

I've blocked out the rest of that meal, except that Karly and I split the tab, since we were the only club members in our tribe. Then JOURNEY-MAN thanked me for dinner and gave me a tender kiss.

That had calmed me down—until I saw Solange slip her business card into his hand while we waited for the valet to bring our cars to the clubhouse entrance. When they smiled, I could feel the sparks between them, and I felt betrayed by both guests of our tribe.

Nonnie must've watched Solange's play for JOURNEYMAN because she leaned closer to me and whispered, "He's going home with you. Make him glad he did."

I'll shut that Belle de Jour out of my thoughts, I said to myself.

We'd barely walked into my bedroom when the old competitive spirit inspired my wild woman to win his heart that night—like it had during breakup sex with Walter.

Whoa. Is that what I just had with JOURNEYMAN before he turns to Solange? Don't even think it. I can't help it. Their attraction's a runaway train that can't be stopped. Will he have the balls to tell me he moved on?

I almost woke him to ask him, but I stopped myself. I had to put a stop sign on each jealous thought that came to mind, so I could calm down and fall asleep. The last time I looked at the clock, it was 3:34.

Six hours later, I was driving a golf cart on my high-mountain desert course, watching JOURNEYMAN play it like a pro.

After his birdie on the longest hole, he seemed to be speaking from his heart when he said, "Come home with me."

"Before Solange moves in?" I disliked my high-pitched voice of fear.

He squeezed my right knee, "I feel safe with you."

"I don't feel safe while she's after you," I said, wishing my fear would stop shouting so I could hear what he was telling me.

"I'd choose a woman like you, over a spoiled girl."

I took a breath and let that sink in. "An ounce of woman's worth a pound of girl?" His grin encouraged me. "See how I turn life into lyrics?"

"When your songs go platinum, you'll need the best financial advisor around."

"You're my guy." I wanted to stop on a positive note, but I couldn't. "Unless Solange gets her way."

"You're obsessed with her," he said, sounding annoyed.

"When things get crowded, I run. I won't survive that torture again."

He nodded and finished his last few holes in silence. He acted like he was concentrating on his game, but it felt like he'd shut me out. I knew I might have gone overboard, blabbing my fears. But I thought he was rude, although I didn't complain, when he made a cell call that lasted the whole time I drove him to the Santa Fe airport, where his sleek white jet was waiting for him.

I walked with him onto the lonesome tarmac, where we kissed politely. He pulled away without any mention of meeting again. Turning toward his jet, he answered his cell phone as he climbed the stairs. This was my last chance to give him my gift.

"I love you," I said.

He paused a split second, as if it had registered. Then he stepped inside the plane without looking back. My heart took a nosedive, as I ran to my car and sped away.

My fast escape stirred up dust that clouded my view of his jet. I swallowed a wave of emotion, and my heart clenched. Thankfully, I was heading to see Doctor G for a quick check up before I drove to Albuquerque Sun Port.

Sitting on the treatment table with my head bowed, I didn't see Doctor G walk up to me. "Where does it hurt?" he asked.

I held my chest. "Pain means stop," I whispered.

"Stop, look and listen, so you know what needs correcting," Doctor G said.

"I will not love a Pioneer." I looked up and caught his gaze, "So my heart won't break again."

Doctor G patted my head, and his kindness triggered my silent sob.

I didn't understand the body-shaking depth of my sadness, but it showed me a bright side. "At least my back doesn't hurt," I said.

Handing me a tissue for my tears, he said, "It should hold up until I get my hands on you again in a few weeks. Your heart needs more attention."

"Who's doesn't," I muttered.

He checked my wrist pulses and tested some supplements to find *the chosen few* that strengthened me. Then he emptied a few capsules onto my tongue and gave me a cup of water as a chaser.

"I rarely offer personal advice," Doctor G said. "But I hope you won't settle down until you finish growing into the magnificent woman you're becoming—even if it takes several more years on your own."

"I'm not ready to be a Settler," I said. *Neither is JOURNEYMAN.*

8. LETTING GO

The airport taxi dropped me off at home after nine, and I hoped for welcome-home hugs from my children. Instead, I followed the sound of Rocky Balboa beating up a slab of ribs downstairs and found Logan attacking the punching bag with his bare fists.

When I asked what was wrong, he waved me away, venting more rage against that leather bag. I was stunned to see my kind-hearted son in such a state, but I didn't know how to help him.

I turned on a trail of lights leading upstairs to my room, and waited for him to follow. On my way there, I'd noticed Jade had gone to sleep an hour earlier than usual. I listened to some voicemail messages and wrote in my journal until I heard the pummeling stop in our basement gym.

Leaning into my bedroom doorway a minute later, Logan still looked red and raw. "I know why you threw plates at Dad."

"At the floor, not your dad," I blurted, instantly realizing I'd missed his point.

"I've known her two months, not twenty years." Logan left before I could summon any words of comfort. *I never wanted him to know that pain.*

The phone woke me from a restless sleep at six the next morning—would I sub for the Language Arts teacher? I tested my back and it felt fine, so I accepted the assignment.

By 6:30, I'd packed brown-bag lunches and set three plates of eggs with veggies on the table, when Logan sat down and tossed his sample bag on the floor.

I told him, "A knife in the heart hurts the same in any time frame."

Joining us in her burgundy plaid uniform, Jade asked, "A Cutco knife?"

Logan's glare said, *Drop it.* Wisely, she did.

While we ate, I wondered aloud why Lily was curled up in the corner instead of begging for food. They told me the only thing she ate was pizza on Logan's poker night. That concerned me, but Jade drew my focus away from Lily. "Our show at the Rec Center is sold out tonight," Jade said.

"On a school night?" I asked.

"It ends at nine," she said. "Dad and Marcy are coming. Is that a problem?"

I cringed, but rose above my discomfort. "That's two more fans of your music."

Jade said she could get us in for free, and we accepted her offer. As I headed upstairs to change into *teacher clothes,* something made me say, "Give Lily a hug before you leave."

When I returned to the kitchen ten minutes later, I stopped at the dishwasher, watching soap suds ooze out of it. *Boot camp will continue,* I thought, as I cleaned up their well-intended effort. Then I took a short cut to school on the toll road.

My first day back in the classroom, a few weeks after my injury, was pain free—unlike the decision I'd have to make later that day.

After school, I gave Lily a bird-shaped biscuit and cuddled her while she chomped on it. When I saw blood dripping out of her mouth, I thought she broke a tooth. When I saw a puddle of blood by her tail, things went into slow motion.

Somehow, I hoisted Lily onto an old Navaho blanket in my car and drove her to see the new Emergency Vet with the kind smile. Once again, nobody else was in his waiting room; so he examined her right away.

"I could do surgery on her ruptured tumors, but she may not survive it," he said. "There's the alternative we talked about. Want to call your husband, or anyone?"

I shook my head. Then I looked into Lily's eyes, which showed no sign of enthusiasm or resistance. "We're ready," I said.

The soft-spoken Vet gave me the option of being present or not, so I held Lily while I let her go. She nestled her nose in my breast, like she did when I first held her as a pup. This time, she must have sensed sorrow in my heartbeats.

Cradling her for less than a minute, I felt energetic bursts of her breath. After a few years of wheezing, her final breaths were sweet sounds of relief. She drifted to sleep hearing my voice. "Thanks for loving us, Lily. And for keeping us safe. Thank you."

I heard the Vet quietly wrap up his gear before he left the room, saying I could stay with her as long as I wanted. I tucked her limp body into our Navaho blanket and hugged her one last time before I left.

Numb. That's how I felt as I sat quietly at my kitchen table, watching darkness unfold. When Logan, Jade and her band came home after their concert, they headed to the refrigerator, as usual. It's light jarred me, and they jumped when they saw me.

Jade turned on the overhead lights and glared at me, "You said you'd come tonight."

I couldn't speak. Logan understood. "Lily?"

I nodded, and my tears welled up for the first time as reality hit hard.

"Band hug," said Bert, the male lead singer.

As they silently huddled around me, I gave them some good news. "She breathed like a pup again, as she went to sleep in my arms."

Bert said, "She looked like walking death for months."

Logan patted my head. "You're the only one who couldn't see it."

"Let's get a new yellow dog," Jade said.

I gasped at the thought of raising a new pup. "My head's pounding. I'm going upstairs," I said. While soaking in a bubble bath, candlelight and Pachebel Canon in D, I left voicemails of this sad news with my dog-lover friends.

Sharon was the first to return my call and offer her sympathy. I thanked her and remembered what I needed to do. "Are you seeing anyone?" I asked.

"I'm waiting for my Pioneer to come back," Sharon said. "Even if it's just for great sex."

"Let him go," I said.

"Have you heard something?" Sharon asked.

"He met someone in Santa Fe."

"How do you know?"

"I was with him, but I'm afraid he already moved on to greener trails."

Sharon shrieked, "I told you not to go out with him."

"We waited," I said. "He assured me you two were through. You set up John before we were through."

"Don't you dare contact me again," Sharon said, with seething intensity.

She slammed down her phone before I could speak. Splash. I dunked my throbbing head in hot water. Seconds later, I heard my cell phone vibrate on my marble tub. Surfacing for air, I answered it.

"Sorry about Lily," JOURNEYMAN said.

Eerie timing, **I thought.** With high-pitched sadness, I shared the details of losing Lily and now Sharon.

"You're strong, Hadley," he said. "You'll get through this. I'll call you next week."

Splash. I did another partial back float in the tub. A few minutes later, my float was interrupted by an unexpected caller. It was Walter, who kept saying he was sorry I lost Lily. I kept thanking him, until I realized what he really wanted and I gave it to him.

"I'm sorry you lost her, too."

Walter cleared his throat, "Thank you." Click.

His sadness compounded mine, so I escaped with a leftover pain pill and a long sleep.

SPIRITRIDER returned my call a few days later. Instead of the usual greeting, he announced, "I'm done with crazy love."

For now, I thought. "So you're taking care of yourself."

"Who's taking care of you without Lily snuggled at your feet?"

Since I was writing at my desk where I felt her absence the most, I told him my antidote. "I already called her breeder to buy a pup who's related to her."

"Don't buy a rebound puppy," he said, "until you're ready to settle down again."

"Who knows where I'll end up?" I said. "That used to scare me, but now it's exciting."

"You're a new woman. And I'm a new man," he said. "I'm over my addiction to that girl and ready to be with someone I could enjoy life with in thirty years. Like a dear friend."

So he can't be addicted to me? "Friendship can catch fire. Hopefully."

"Not in my experience," he said. "But I wasn't open to that idea until now."

Since we were in a confiding mood, I told him about the Sharon situation and asked for his take on it.

"She didn't have a contract, so he was a free agent," he said.

He thinks like JOURNEYMAN. "But how do I make things right, if she won't take my calls?"

"She'll come around," SPIRITRIDER said. "Until then, focus on other friends, like me. Too bad we don't live closer, Hadley girl. We could have some fun."

My wild woman perked up. "That's true," I said. "Let's stay in touch."

A week later, I received, "A message from the animal hospital." That was my Vet's code—which meant Lily's ashes were ready for pick up. I stopped by the next morning before school, arriving a few steps behind my new Vet, who held the door for me.

I was about to re-introduce myself when he said, "I'm sorry for your loss, Mrs. Finch."

I nodded. "You must work day and night shifts."

"It's my startup. I live upstairs," he said. His reception area was vacant again, when he picked up a small box and offered it like a Tiffany treasure on a velvet tray.

It was heavier than I'd imagined, holding Lily's dust in my hands. "Thank you, Doctor—"

"Mitchell. Remember that name," he said.

"I'll send you some customers," I said, as I left his waiting room.

The next week, it was time for my second back treatment with Doctor G. My back was holding up well when I flew to Albuquerque with Logan and Jade, so the first thing we did was head to our favorite mountain trail to fulfill another purpose of our trip.

While we hiked up a rocky path, dotted with summer wildflowers, Jade asked, "Do we call the mountain gods?"

"Not today," I said.

During this gentle hike with my children, I was picturing family hikes that Lily had led throughout their growing-up years, always ending with a splash in *Lily's Stream*. On our final hike with Lily, we held onto her tin urn and freed her ashes on wings of a breeze that carried her into a long embrace with her stream.

The timing of our memorial mission was beyond coincidence. It was a revelation. On the way home from the mountain, while we shared fish tacos and lamb quesadillas on the Coyote's roof-top cantina, I was astonished to see my *Mountain Man* walk in.

I tried to catch his attention with a wave, until I saw Solange join him at their table. I started trembling, and I couldn't hide it.

"Did he jerk you around?" Logan asked.

I shook my head. "An upsetting day." Excusing myself, I walked toward the restroom and heard JOURNEYMAN ask me to wait for him.

He caught up to me at the top of the stairs. "Hi, SONGBIRD."

Turning to face him, I leapt into my yellow-dog mode. "I want you to be happy," I said. "It's your one and only life, so go for it."

"You're really not confrontational, are you?" He watched my emotional shrug and said, "Solange needed an investor."

"It's just business?" I'd used that edgy tone when I'd asked Walter about Tina.

JOURNEYMAN let a few faux cowboys walk past before he said, "It's best if I'm not in a relationship, until I know what I want."

"A French pastry?" *Whoa. I'm humiliating myself.*

"A dangerous woman is a magnet," he whispered, like his defense was a defect.

"What does a dangerous woman do?" I asked.

"The opposite of you," he said.   When I gasped, it threw him off balance. "Not a healthy choice, I know, Hadley."

I raced down the stairs and into the rest room with one thought on my mind: *I will not love a Pioneer.* I repeated it until I regained my composure. When I returned to my children I saw that his table was empty. *The Pioneer left with his pastry.*

"Mr. Murphy came over to say *Hi*," Jade said. "Who is he?"

"A good man," I said.

"Not good enough for our mooti," Logan said, and Jade nodded.

Focusing on their support helped me erase him from my thoughts.

The next morning, I'd scheduled wellness visits for Logan and Jade, so Doctor G could tune up their body chemistry and alignment. Then I sent them to town for an hour, while I received a round of shots in my lower back.

During my deep breathing on the treatment table, I sent my mind back to our soothing mountain trail, where spring buds were maturing into summer blooms. *Like my hopes for loving JOURNEYMAN, turning into lessons about trust, resilience.*

Right after my injections, as Doctor G watched me do the bicycle exercise to get the fresh fluid moving into my discs, he asked what else was troubling me. I didn't want to sound like Lady Gueneviere, who couldn't let go of Lancelot, so I mentioned something that Doctor G might be able to fix. "I started snoring."

"The sounds of an earthy woman," he said.

"My engine noise woke me up. I wouldn't inflict that on anyone," I said. *If JOURNEYMAN heard it, no wonder he moved on.*

"We're working on blood sugar and thyroid issues which contribute to snoring," he said. "It takes time to correct."

"No more sleepovers until it's fixed," I said, blurting my true concerns.

Doctor G asked if I could handle a little more discomfort. After I nodded, he put on latex gloves and adjusted the roof of my mouth with intense fingertip pressure. During each of a dozen slow pushes, a stream of tears flowed down my cheeks, and air started flowing through both nostrils again.

Afterwards, he patted my cheeks with a tissue. "It may not stay fixed until we correct your chemistry." When I hid my face behind my hands, he asked, "What else is stressing you?"

I sat upright on his table. "I will not love a Pioneer," I said. "My new mantra."

"A better mantra would be, I am cherished by the Great Father," he said. "Once you believe that, you'll only desire a man who nurtures and adores you. And you'll take appropriate action, which works better than any mantra."

I thanked Doctor G with a hug and felt his $1,300 bill for a day of wellness and daily supplements for my whole family was worth every cent.

Once again, my step was lighter as I left his office and headed to the library near the plaza to use the computer. Printing three e-boarding passes for our Southwest flight home, I felt lucky we'd made it into GROUP A.

> I had a few minutes before Logan and Jade would meet me there, so I checked my emails and felt even luckier when I read:

> **"Dear SONGBIRD, Are you known in real life by the name of a songbird? If so, I joined SOULFULDATES to get to know you. I don't do video chats, because I keep a low profile for business reasons. I also write music, so we have a lot in common. Hope to hear from you. PETLOVR4U"**

I was still recharging my emotional battery after JOUR-NEYMAN, so my first impulse was to look for reasons to say, *No. Boring*, my wild woman told me. *Say YES and see what develops—the way you improvised scenes in the good old days. Go for it, Hadley girl.*

"Dear PETLOVR4U, Yes, I'm known by the name of a songbird, and I'm honored you joined this site to meet me. Your baseball cap hid your face, but I liked what you wrote and I'd like to meet you. How about Joyful Café this Saturday at ten? SONGBIRD"

On a fateful Saturday in June, I arrived at Joyful Café a few minutes early. In the midst of a dozen people waiting to get inside, I saw a familiar face in the crowd.

Feeling my heart beat faster, I said, "It's you."

PETLOVR kissed my hand. "I wanted to do that the first time I saw you, Mrs. Finch. The day Lily led you to the last great love of your lifetime."

No longer a mild-mannered Emergency Vet in my eyes, I now saw a Super Settler standing before me. And I felt too electrified to speak.

"Let's go." He took my hand and led me on a walk toward an Ice Rink with snow piled outside. "The first time I looked in your eyes, I wanted to stay there forever," he said. "When I saw how you cared for Lily—well I knew it was love."

"Don't you mean *serious like?*"

He smiled. "I mean head-over-heels, stop-seeing-anyone-else-love."

"Isn't that premature infatuation?" I teased.

We followed a cinder trail that wound through an industrial complex as PETLOVR said, "It's real love, like I've never felt before. I love my two kids. My in-laws. My wife, as a friend. But you're the one I've hoped to find for years. So I'm done looking. I hope you are, too."

He sounds like a Super Settler, except for one thing, "You mean your ex- wife?"

"Our divorce is signed and ready for a Judge's approval next month," he said. "We're in separate bedrooms. She's moving out with our 16 year old twins."

"You must've had babies in your early twenties."

He nodded. "The end of our sex life. She was a caring pal for 17 years."

I walked backwards, so I could watch his reaction. "When I heard that from a few men I met through *The Lunch Bunch*, I didn't believe a sexless marriage could last."

"It can," he said. "My kids are old enough, so I can think of my needs."

"Have you had your rebound relationship?"

"I don't need one," he said. "I know what I want. And it's you."

I didn't know how to handle his certainty. But I certainly knew how much of his energy and focus would be needed to help his whole family bloom again after their big breakup. "What if I asked you to get your divorce and call me in a year?"

"You'd be walking away from the greatest love affair of the 21st century."

Poor pup. Looks like he believes his own line. "I'd like one in this century, since I had one in the last."

"Impossible. Or you wouldn't be here. Me either, if I'd found it with my wife."

I stopped on a beam of light streaming through a canopy of elm trees. "Found what?" I asked, letting his guileless charm draw me closer.

"I won't tell you, I'll—" he said, moving closer like he wanted to kiss me.

I wanted to let him, but I pulled back. "Not while you're living with your wife."

"She started dating and said I should too," he said. "I wasn't ready until I saw you. But you were so focused on Lily, you didn't see me. Until now."

"You're a perceptive PETLOVR," I said.

"Do I need a note from my wife, before I take you to dinner Saturday?"

His cheerful optimism and the sweet sparkle in his eyes helped me decide. "I'll trust you," I said. Then he did a little dance that made me laugh.

9. THE BIG BANG

"Do you have a piano?" That was PETLOVR's first question to me on Saturday evening, while he greeted me with a bear hug in my foyer.

He'd already started to feel like a dear friend, thanks to hours we'd spent chatting on the phone while he'd waited in vain for emergency cases to show up at his new animal hospital.

"Mention it on the dating site, and you'll have plenty of PETLOVRS-4-U," I'd suggested.

"I got off the site after I found you, but I see SONGBIRD's still active."

"You're still living with your wife. No exclusive dating, until you're legally free again," I'd said. PETLOVR accepted that boundary by phone.

Now I was eager to see how we felt about each other on our second date. I led him into my music room where he sat down at my hand-carved concert grand piano with reverent delight.

"A Knabe," he said. He stretched his fingers and played a tune that sounded like a new-age number by Yanni. When PETLOVR reached a moving climax, I saw tears in his eyes. His exhale was tinged with a sigh, "I wrote that for my mom. She died this winter."

BAM. *He broke through the wall around my heart. No. The impact's greater. It's more like a big bang that exploded within itself and created an ever-expanding universe of possibilities.* "You're her legacy of love," I said.

He pressed his fingertips against mine and folded our hands together like a child's hands in prayer. "I want to know you and what's in your heart," he said. "If it takes 50 years, that's fine by me."

"Are you too good to be true?"

He shook his head. "I'm real."

I looked at his lips in a way that invited his first kiss. "Soft lips," I sighed.

He whispered back, "I want to date you with an eye toward marriage."

"Hmm," I said, noticing how he'd inspired my wild woman to guide his hands off the ivories, beneath my summer skirt, onto my bare thighs. The touch of his fingertips was a torch I could've let burn—if we weren't rattled when keys clanged in the front door.

"I'm home," Jade announced.

We straightened up in the few seconds it took her to find us at the piano.

"Oh, hi guys. My mom said you helped Lily at the end."

"Your mom helped more." He stood and offered his hand. "I'm Doctor Mitchell."

I got up to speed. "And this is my daughter, Jade."

Accepting his strong handshake, she said, "Sweaty hands. Did you just play?"

He turned to me and his face went blank, so I answered, "He just played a lovely song he wrote. Have you written others, Doctor Mitchell?"

"Matthew," he said. "I've written dozens. When I was your age, Jade, I had to choose between Julliard or Vet school. So my music is still in me. It's good you're sharing yours."

"Thanks," Jade said. Then she asked to see me in the kitchen for a minute. I followed her there and asked what was on her mind.

"He still looks good for an old guy," she said.

"He's a lot younger than I am."

"And he likes you. Go have fun without figuring out what's wrong with him."

"You think I'm too critical?"

"With men. That's why you're not dating anyone."

"I'll give that some thought. Thanks, " I said. She gave me her proud smile.

Matthew Mitchell and I chose a garden table at a local French bistro, Mon Ami Gabi, where crickets provided background music on that steamy

June night. He ordered a reasonable-but-lovely bottle of Bordeaux that I'd recommended.

Lifting his goblet, he said, "It's our first meal as a couple, Sweetie Pie—"

He's got to be kidding. "I like SONGBIRD. Or Hadley girl."

"To my sweet SONGBIRD. I know this is our first night of forever, so—"

"Whoa. I know I'm wonderful, but I don't know anything about you."

"All we needed to know was in our kiss," he said.

I laughed, until I noticed his puzzled look. "What about shared values and strong PIES—Physical-Intellectual-Emotional-Spiritual health?" I asked.

"After a cold marriage, I want hot chemistry. The rest is details." He touched my hand, and I felt a surge of pleasure that I wouldn't spoil with a debate.

While sharing tastes of his lamb and my beef burgundy, I asked about the women in his life. His revelations flowed as freely as a leaf on the summer breeze. His mother was a teacher. She'd made a joyful but frugal home after his father died in a motorcycle accident thirty years ago—on his eighth birthday.

"I'll grow old a decade before you," I blurted, then winced for not expressing sympathy for losing his dad so young—before I brought up our age difference.

"You'll never grow old, 'cause you love and trust," he said.

Luckily, our table was surrounded by trees, because I planted a kiss that could have gotten us thrown out of there. When I settled down, he cradled my hands at his chest. "I like your wild side," he said.

"It's the key to my success in my life and art, if you believe my birth chart that SPIRITRIDER sent me."

PETLOVR told me he had a wild side in college and gave me proof. He'd chatted up two divorcees at a beach in Cancun over spring break senior year. A month later, they tracked him down in his fraternity house, and the threesome spent 24 hours driving each other wild. They made so much racket that his frat brothers bowed at the sight of him for days.

"It's good to bring back parts of us that we've lost," I said. "But that kind of wild side is dynamite to your marriage."

"Don't worry," he said, as if he understood my concern. "I stayed faithful for 17 years of family love, even without passion. My wife asked for a divorce the day after my mom died, so she wouldn't upset her. I've been humbled."

He seemed genuinely moved, so I said, "You've been cheated. It's catch-up time."

The waiter served our espressos; then PETLOVR leaned closer. "Besides chemistry, my needs in a partner are simple," he said. "Love and respect of animals, kids, music and each other. With you, I get all that and more, wrapped up in a blonde bombshell."

He didn't crack a smile. "Don't you want to date around before you settle down?"

He shook his head. "I don't want to become an old pro, who does the same old—same old, for years. I'm more turned on by you than I ever was before. So let's stay focused on what we've got. Savor it, like this wine. Except—"

My puzzled look asked him to continue. "You're a dangerous woman."

I beamed at the sound of that. "How so?"

"You get me talking. You ask questions and make me open up."

I loved his definition, but I wondered aloud, "And that scares you?"

He nodded. "I've been known to say things without thinking first."

"Total transparency is good," I said. "What comes into your mind comes out of your mouth. That's how we improvised scenes onstage."

"I might have to try that, if my current business doesn't catch on fast."

I thought that might be his cue to pick up our dinner tab, so I reached for it. He took it away from me. "My treat, SONGBIRD. My pleasure."

As thanks, I offered to cook dinner for him on his only night off the next week.

Before I met PETLOVR again, I called Max at her news desk with one quick question. "Would you believe a younger guy who talks forever on the first date?"

"Some men say anything to get some," Max said. "Can't blame him for trying or you for wanting some. But if you believe him, I'll have to slap some sense in you, girl." Click.

Hmm. That's what I thought. I have to trust my instincts.

On Thursday evening, PETLOVR joined me for buffalo burgers in my tropical garden, while Jade's band music seeped out of the basement during practice. When he found out Logan couldn't join us because he was playing rat hockey later that night, he asked if he could play with Logan next time.

"You play hockey?" I asked, amazed he had common interests with both of my kids.

He nodded. "So do my twins, who'll be right at home here on weekends once we're married."

Time for a reality check. "How's your divorce coming?"

"I told you, I'll be a free man soon."

I remembered Walter's warning to me outside Divorce Court on D-Day: "You're house rich, Hadley. Men will love you for your lifestyle. Don't mix marriage and money," he'd said.

In hindsight, I could see how Walter's divorce deal had protected me from that scenario. Since PETLOVR kept mentioning marriage, it was time to give him my financial love test.

"I should tell you my divorce support runs several more years, unless I remarry."

Filling his dessert dish with berries and cream, he looked up. Then he shook his head. "I had a thought, but it might not send the right message to our children," he said.

It's easy to read his mind. "You mean living together?" He nodded, and I said, "My support would stop. Don't you think that's fair?"

He drizzled cream on my berries and asked, "Substantial support?"

"I couldn't run my homes without it."

"You can't walk away from that." He scanned fiery remnants of the sunset then he swatted the table. "Holy Shit. You could be a grandmother before I could marry you."

My *reality check*. "Or I write a hit song. Or we enjoy each other's company without a legal merger."

He jiggled his leg nervously. "If you just want hedonistic kicks, I'm not your guy."

"If you want a nurse and a purse, I'm not your gal."

Watching his peels of laughter, I thought he looked guilty. "Busted?"

"You think I wouldn't sign a pre-nup, silly lady? I'd like you to know something important about me," he said, leaning closer, like he was about to share a secret. With his fingertips, he feathered my cheekbones. "I think I could love you, in spite of all these little lines on your face."

That verbal slap made me gasp. He sounded defensive. "I'm trying to see past them. You're beautiful inside."

My mind swelled with second thoughts. "You're free to be with a girl. I see the appeal. No signs of life happening to her yet."

"A girl means more babies. Why go backwards?" He tugged at my belt buckle, "I bet we'd be a great fit. Let's go find out," he said.

The sexual edge in his voice nearly erased his slap. I was firm, "Not with children home."

"I have a car," he whispered.

That gave my wild woman an idea. I slid the linen cloth off my table without breaking our dessert bowls, and I grabbed his hand. His grin said he was game, so we trotted over a few manicured acres, into an overgrown yard of a brick ranch. It was wrapped in tarps while a second story was being built. *Looks like the coast is clear.*

Camouflaged by weeping willows and an unfolding blanket of darkness, we jumped on a squeaky trampoline and landed on our bouncy bed. Tucked beneath our tablecloth, we shared some laughter and kisses that easily could've jumpstarted a relationship.

Until a beam of light got our attention through our veil, and a craggy male voice shouted, "No trespassing."

"Do your parents know what you're doing?" asked an older woman, as she tugged at our cloth.

"We are parents," I said, disguising my voice in a serious tone. "And I didn't know you lived here during construction. Sorry."

"Mrs. Finch? Is that you under there?" she asked.

Damn. "Could you give me a hall pass, Mrs. Feller, and keep this between us?"

Mr. Feller growled, "Next time we send the Dobermans."

PETLOVER spoke up from undercover. "How about a little privacy, Fellers."

I poked him, and he tickled me. "We're leaving," I squealed. "When you turn off your light." Click.

In the darkness, wrapped in our tablecloth with my push-up bra dangling below my blouse, we scooted off the trampoline and I heard Mrs. Feller shout, "He's not your husband."

I faced my accuser. "Haven't you heard? Walter left me, and—"

PETLOVR pulled me away before I could explain. As we dashed through their overgrown lawn, I heard Mr. Feller say to his wife, "Be nice to me. Or you'll end up like her."

Whoa. He doesn't bring out the best in me.

As we climbed the rail-tie stairway to my back deck, he said, "I like the way you ended up." A minute later, he repeated that, adding a sweet kiss. Then he hopped into his rusty car and leaned out the window for another kiss. I obliged.

"I never did this stuff in school. Or in my marriage," I said.

"So I'm good for you. Remember that." He blew me a kiss as he drove away.

A fun way to look at it. Fun is what Walter said he wanted when he left me. Is this the kind of fun he had with Tina? Who cares? It's about ME now.

PETLOVR's wife was supposed to end up like me in divorce court the following week. Since he'd found a Vet to cover both shifts for him on his D-Day, I prepared a picnic dinner so we could mark his big milestone together in a tranquil setting—at the bath and tennis club where I'd stayed in shape for twenty summers.

He arrived an hour late at our sign-in desk. I gave him a red rose, and he tossed it over his shoulder. "You don't like your freedom?" I asked.

"The Judge threw out the deal we already signed. Called it unconscionable. If I don't fight, I'll have to pay her more than she's worth."

Don't make me say, NEXT, Buster. "I wrote a whole album about the *Value Of A Woman*, after I barely survived the court battle over it. I don't choose to go through that again."

"Then we won't talk about it," he said.

After a pack of soggy swimmers sloshed past us, I said, "We'll talk about it once. Tonight. To see if what I learned can help you. Then we won't talk to each other again, until you work it out with her." My new boundary startled both of us.

Rubbing his forehead, he said, "It could take months. You could fall for someone else."

I held his sweaty hand. "It's not falling. It's planting seeds in solid ground—"

He wasn't listening. I saw his hot-tempered kick of the dirt and thought of a way he could cool down. I led him to a wooden dock by a spring-fed pond, where I asked him to explain his divorce deal.

He did, while we donned life jackets over our swimsuits and paddled around the pond in privacy. When he finished putting his rosy spin on his deal, I said, "I see what's wrong. You're generous with your kids but cheap with your wife." Then I suggested a few affordable ways to be fair to her, like giving her a cut of his profits for a few years after his new animal hospital takes off.

"But she's the one who wanted out," he said, with a boyish pout.

A new rhyme popped to mind. "Happy ex-wife. Happy new life."

His cheeks turned red, and then he paddled toward the gushing fountain in the center of the pond. "Whoopie," I cheered.

As I let the fountain spray wash my cares away, a lifeguard shouted on his megaphone. "Get away from the fountain, Mrs. Finch, or no boating the rest of the summer."

I shrugged, and PETLOVR said we could take his boat on the lake all summer.

Blocking the pounding spray with my hands, I said, "Uh-huh. Bigger boats make me sick."

"I want to live on a boat and travel the world when I retire," he whined.

"Good luck," I said in a dismissive tone.

Dirty water was rising up to our ankles, when we grabbed a paddle and started bailing. The teenage lifeguard rowed up and helped us into his boat as ours was sinking. I apologized to the guard, who kept shaking his head while he took us back to the dock.

As we stepped onto solid ground, PETLOVR sounded confident, "We can work this out."

I had my doubts. But I wouldn't let them spoil the special picnic I'd spent the afternoon preparing. We went into the girls and boys rooms to shower and change into dry clothes. Then we dined on the banks of our pond, overlooking our sunken rowboat and the setting sun.

While sharing a bottle of Clos du Val and a wild halibut, roasted veggie picnic, we hardly said a word to each other. "We were hungry," I said, offering a graceful excuse for our silence. It expired after we ate every bite of dinner.

His eyes welled up. "I already care about you, SONGBIRD. If your heart was divided, I couldn't take it. I'd have to move on."

A *welcome change from a Pioneer*, I thought. Then I reconsidered our boundary. "What if we see each other as soon as your wife moves out?"

He bowed his head, and I felt misgivings. "I don't want to lose you to the next woman you meet," I said. "But I run from anything that reminds me how my marriage blew up."

"That old baggage stops you from loving me," he said.

"You're a perceptive PETLOVR," I said, stretching onto my side to face him. "My motto for you."

He touched my calf, gliding his fingertips up to my knee. "You're divorced a few years, but in many ways I'm further along than you are."

"Because you didn't have a passionate marriage. That's hard to lose. Hard to find again."

"Could you find it with me?" He played a pretend piano tune on my inner thigh, and a surge of excitement propelled me toward our first kiss. I knew that was a big risk.

As I'd imagined and even hoped, his heart was so hungry after 17 years of starvation, that one kiss quickly escalated into a carnal feast under our blanket.

In our decisive moment, he put on the brakes. "Will you respect me after?"

That was so unexpected, I had to laugh. "Isn't that the woman's question?"

"I'm serious," he said, kneeling upright on the lawn. "I'm in this for the long haul, so I won't put the cart before the horse. I don't think you want it enough—yet."

I opened my picnic basket and showed him the packets of protection I'd brought along. When he grinned, I grabbed his belt buckle and whispered, "Giddyup." When he did, my initial thoughts justified the risk. *It's dark. No one can see us or hear us. What's the harm of enjoying each other under the stars?*

I looked up at PETLOVER, shouldering our *pup tent*, speed-humping with his eyes closed in a grinning trance. *He's off on a good vacation to a strange land, but he's left me behind.* I touched his eyelids, yet I couldn't engage him. *Oh, well.*

Closing my eyes, I drifted into my own pleasure place, losing track of time and space. It was dark when we eased into a new awareness of our separate selves. Not a moment too soon.

"Can I see your IDs?" an alto voice asked us.

Damn. We sat up, holding the blanket against us. A man in uniform stood beside us, shining a flashlight on his badge, then into our faces. PETLOVR handed over his ID. I told him my purse was in my car.

Blinding me with his light, he asked, "How old are you?"

"I don't tell my age," I said, and PETLOVR covered up his groan with a cough.

"What about your name? Would you tell me that?" the Officer asked.

That's even worse. I won't be able to show my face in this town if this news gets around, I thought. "I'm over 21 and a good citizen. Same for my friend."

"Not married, hey?" the Officer said.

"We've got kids and a wife at home, so no privacy," PETLOVR said in a tone that asked for some understanding.

"Ex-wife, soon," I said. "But not because of us."

"Nobody's allowed here after dark," the Officer said. "So get going, and have a good night."

We thanked him, and when he walked out of earshot, I groaned, "Look what I do, under your influence."

"You're a blast," he said. I saw delight in his eyes, as he plucked twigs and blades of grass out of my tangled hair.

When PETLOVR helped me pack up my car in the lot, he said, "That guy had to run our plates. Wait till he tells the gang about the hot grannie caught in the act with her young stud."

That big slap made me want to smack him, but I had better communication skills. "Are you a klutz or a bastard?"

His eyes opened wide. "You don't like my joke?"

"If you're defending it, go find a young studette."

"You mean a trophy wife? I could have one, but I don't want one. I want you."

Three slaps and he's out. "If I'm not your trophy, we're through," I said. Then I jumped into my car and sped out of the parking lot without glancing back.

During my drive home, I felt lost, like my chord had been cut from the mother ship and I had to grab hold before I floated away. In that weakened state, I walked in my dark house and went straight to my computer.

Logging into my dating site, I clicked on PETLOVR and saw he was ONLINE NOW. *He's already hunting for someone new. No Mulligans allowed?*

Without thinking, I clicked on JOURNEYMAN's profile and saw he'd been active on the site within 24 hours. *He must've moved on from Solange.* I dashed off an e-mail, asking if he wanted to catch up. I did the same with SPIRITRIDER and SEEKER007. Only then did I realize I'd be stepping backwards if I reconnected with them. *I want to move forward.*

For the first time since I joined the dating site four or five months ago, I took a giant step forward. I tried on the female hunter role and launched a search for men, 45 to 55 years old, who lived within 5000 miles of my zip code.

Voila! Within a few seconds, a fifty-page catalogue of SOULFULDATES appeared for my viewing pleasure, with ten men pictured on each page. I scanned the menu of men, waiting for one to catch my eye.

"Are you cheating on Matthew?" Jade asked, arriving without a sound.

I sat up in a pose that blocked her view of my screen. "It's complicated."

"Stop looking," Jade said. "There's nobody better for you. And I always wanted a stepfather who's into music and wants to spend time with us."

Did it feel like her dad's been gone that long? "I just broke up with him."

While patting my shoulder, she said, "Un-break up with him."

"Why mess up my life?"

"So you won't be alone when I leave home."

She'd mentioned this before, so I had to do a better job of launching her. "I'll see what I can accomplish on my own. So will you. No need to worry about me."

"Will you worry about me, Mom?"

"I only send you positive thoughts and love. Would you do that for me?"

Jade nodded and asked if a few friends could sleep over. Permission granted, she ran outside to join them on the trampoline. She couldn't possibly have known how she'd helped me refocus. When I looked back at the menu of men, I'd lost my appetite for meeting someone new. I hid my dating profile and decided to focus on something more productive.

10. SECOND CHANCES

Coincidentally, a week after I decided to jumpstart my career, I read in the ARTS section of the *TRIBUNE* that a feature film would be shot in Chicago over the next few months. I called my agent, who'd represented me ever since my Miss Teenage America competition when I was sixteen, and asked her if any local actors would be cast in that new film.

Still working two days a week in her 70s, Lois was direct. "How do you look?"

"The same, except thinner than my married days," I said, grateful it was true.

"Then I'll see what I can do," Lois said.

The next week, her business partner and daughter, Laura, called me into her office to tape an audition for a small scene in a big film called *SECOND CHANCES*—about dating after 40.

Standing beside her video camera, looking fit and foxy as a new member of AARP, Laura asked me to describe my recent filmmaking and dating experiences. Then she recorded the monologue I improvised for her camera audience:

> "A few years ago, I starred in a short feature about a jilted wife. I was going through my divorce, so my emotions were raw and right for the character. That could be why I got the part.
>
> At our first cast meeting, the director said she only had the budget to shoot one take of each camera set-up. So we rehearsed each set-up like scenes in a stage play, and we had to deliver the desired emotional goods each time we heard, ACTION—

Only once during filming, when the audio guy lost key dialogue, and the film wouldn't make sense without it, did we get a second chance.

That's like dating at midlife. Lost love is a rehearsal for new love—when we have to deliver the desired emotional goods on take one, or it's *NEXT*. Because time is limited and many wonderful singles would love to take your place or co-star in your love story. It's only when life doesn't make sense without your new love, that we might get a second chance."

That went well, I thought. Then I heard Laura's critique:

"That was a *Donna Reed* monologue for a *Fatal Attraction* kind of character," Laura said. "Sane and eloquent won't get you film work."

"It's not because my age passed my bust size?"

Laura chuckled. "That's changing. Millions of boomers want to see movies about themselves. You're not the only one who got dumped. Who's desperate to date, and see how it's done on screen."

"I'm not desperate. And I don't know how to date. I know how to love."

Laura leaned on the edge of her desk and crossed her arms. "So you couldn't play a suspicious, sex-starved, divorced mom in her 40s?"

I groaned. "That was me—before I found Deepak Chopra and Oprah, and the Dalai Lama turned me into the Dalai Momma."

"Forget about that for this role," Laura said. "Go back to your freaked-out phase during your divorce. That's the gold mine."

Part of me didn't want to go backwards, when my heart clenched day and night. But my wild woman rose to the challenge, eager to turn my old angst into art on the big screen. I told Laura I was ready for *take two*. When I heard *ACTION*, I went back to my danger days:

"When my husband fell for a girl half his age, I was devastated. But I was passionate about winning him back. The nights he left his baby woman to be with me, I wasn't making love with him; I was fighting to save our family. When he left me to go back to her, I was tortured by jealousy and imagined a hundred ways I could whack him and his mistress.

Instead of turning to murder, I put my rage on the page. I let it go in a song, so I could feel whole. One song turned into an album, and—"

Laura interrupted, camera rolling, "Could you love that desperately again? That you'd want to kill a lover who betrayed you?"

I put my hand over my heart. It was racing. So I shook my head.

"Why not?" she asked in an irritated tone.

I tried to answer, but I couldn't swallow the knot in my throat. I watched her click off the video camera.

"Do you want a call back or not?" When I nodded, she coached me. "Could you kill or die for a man's love, because life's worthless without it?"

"That's not true for me, unless I speak as the character."

"Then speak as the character. ACTION."

"I want to love again. But if my lover betrays me, he will be forewarned. Hell hath no fury like a woman scorned. CUT. The rhyme slipped out."

Laura shook her head, as if I failed to make the cut. I was surprised she asked me to get new headshots taken this week so the Studio could see me *all grown up*.

"I'm still growing," I said.

She gave me a photographer's card. "I know it's a big expense for a chance of a few days of work on a film," she said. "If it doesn't pan out, you could start doing industrial training films at SAG scale. It's a nice living."

It's not art, but it'll help pay the bills, I thought as I grabbed the card. Then I booked a shoot on Friday.

I figured that shoot would be a breeze by comparison, when I walked into a loft studio and met a tall, pony-tailed photographer named Evo, short for Evolution. A soft-spoken man of 30, he said he liked my wind-swept look, and he wouldn't change a thing.

Without glancing in a mirror, I sat on a metal bench on a lighted stage and adjusted my navy shirt and white pants. "You want natural, you've got it."

"I want to see you naked. Emotionally," Evo said.

"That's how I've been feeling," I said. "This won't help me snap out of it."

Evo picked up his camera and said softly, "Then think of what makes you feel loved in your most private moments, and let me feel it with you."

His tender tone made me smile, and he took his first shot of me smiling. Then I turned my thoughts inside: *What makes me feel loved? Time with my kids, of course. Privately? Well—moments with JOURNEYMAN. Like our dawn of love on my roof deck. Whoa... I've got to delete him. So... What about PETLOVR? There were glimpses. In our laughter, mostly. On the trampoline. And when he plucked twigs out of my hair. His delight was endearing. He switched. Turned critical, and tried to make me feel old. Whoa. If I think it, my body will live up to it. So I'm forever fit and forty. Yippee!*

"Nice," Evo said. "Thirty-six shots, without coaching."

"That was fun," I said.

Evo hooked up his camera to a monitor and dozens of digital close-ups of my face popped onto the screen. I was shocked. Pointing to shots of my face, I said, "It's unforgiving. I've got my mother's lines."

"Love Lines," Evo said, with a bashful smile.

"You're a sweetheart," I said. "If my dates and directors saw through your lens, I'd be in demand." He nodded, and then we both faced reality. We chose a pose that showed me feeling loved, which downplayed my *love lines. Is that how we erase the years?*

While driving home from Evo's West-Loop studio, I had second thoughts about PETLOVR. *If I'd worn my magnifiers when I looked in the mirror, I would've noticed my lines before he did. What if he wasn't being mean? What if I gave it a negative spin?*

You might say I felt desperate to make things right. When I reached the next fork in the road, I took the path that led me to PETLOVR.

Walking into his empty waiting room, I was planning to tell him about my epiphany, when I saw a young brunette lounging behind the reception desk.

"Oh. Is Doctor Mitchell here?" I asked.

"Do you have an appointment?"

Kind eyes. Good figure. Olive skin. About his age. "Are you Mrs. Mitchell?"

She shook her head. "I'm Doctor Carrera, seeing patients while Doctor Mitchell's away." Glancing down to my feet, she asked, "Where's your pet?"

"When will he be back?" I asked.

She checked her computer screen. "Does Tuesday work for you?"

"I'll check my date book and see." As I left, my thoughts were swirling. *Was it a family vacation? Or did he find a date this fast? Now I've got to spend the 4th of July trying not to think of that while my kids are with their dad. Damn.*

During my drive home, I called Nonnie, like I would've called my mother to tell her what happened and ask for her advice. Only my mother never knew the secret weapons Nonnie shared with me—again:

"When you try *not* to think of something, your mind doesn't read the negative. So that's all you think about," she said. "Now tell me your thinking."

"PETLOVR met a young babe and took her to a hotel for a weekend marathon. Damn him."

"Got evidence?" Nonnie asked.

Turning onto my street, I said, "Nope. If it's my fear talking, it sure feels real."

"If the story you're telling yourself doesn't make you feel great, change it so it does."

"Lie to myself?"

"Change your pattern of thinking that blocks greatness and love," Nonnie said. "See the love under every situation. That's heaven on earth."

Moments later, I found a stairway to heaven when I tuned into the dating site and received this offer:

> **"Dear SONGBIRD, Want to catch up in Ketchem? I'm gathering friends (mostly women) for some hiking and biking. No romance this trip. My plane leaves in two hours. Will you spend the 4th with your friend, JOURNEYMAN?"**
>
> *Would I feel safe?* I wondered. I asked him:
>
> **"Will Solange be at your gathering?"**
>
> **"Solange will not be there. Will you?"**
>
> **"I'd rather fly with you than watch you fly over my car. Where do we meet?"**

What a delightful distraction from PETLOVER, I mused, as I packed my roller-bag.

Climbing the metal stairs that led into JOURNEYMAN'S private jet, I was looking forward to some friendly fun, minus the complications of romance. Once I stepped inside, my jaw dropped.

In the front row, JOURNEYMAN was surrounded by a few girls in their late 20s, who were dressed in skin-tight jeans and skimpy tops. In the row behind him, Max jumped up and gave me a happy squeeze.

"How do you know him?" I asked, as her auburn-haired seat-mate stood up.

"Uh, huh. It's not gonna happen, Scottie. It's Hadley or me," Sharon said.

I hardly recognized her with that new hair color. With a crooked grin, JOURNEYMAN shrugged off her ultimatum. Then he looked at me.

"A sneaky but admirable plan," I said.

Sharon plopped down in her window seat, forcing me to make a choice. *Do I run? Or work through it?* I took the window seat across from Sharon's.

JOURNEYMAN glanced back at me and winked, "Buckle up." Turning to Sharon, he said, "Friends, again?"

I leaned in front of my young seatmate and caught Sharon's gaze. "Our tribe is forever, even if you die your hair red," I said.

"A spirit, not a shade," Max reminded her.

Sharon crossed her arms tighter. "I don't need to forgive without an apology."

"That's the best time. When Walter didn't apologize to me, I did it for him in a song," I said. If she'd seemed receptive, I would've shared a few bars of **Pardon Me**—

> **Pardon me to free yourself from past heartbreak**
> **Pardon me to heal all wounds from my past mistakes**
> **Pardon me please, not my misdeeds**
> **Cross the bridge over anger with my offer of peace.**
> **Choose love over fear. See the best in your friend.**
> **Please pardon me family. Let me love you again—**
> **Pardon Me**

"Forget him. This is about me," Sharon snapped.

I told her what I'd wanted to say for weeks. "I'm sorry."

She nodded. I patted my chest to tell her my heart felt better. She nodded again, and then she looked out her window.

As we made our ascent, I realized JOURNEYMAN had helped our tribe work through the issue that divided us, the way his jet parted the sea of cumulus clouds to reveal blue skies. *Ahhh.*

11. GOOD PIONEER. BAD SETTLER.

As we reached cruising altitude, I leaned against the back of JOURNEYMAN's bucket seat and whispered, "Thanks."

Glancing back at me, he said, "You're brave to come along."

I sat back, thinking *Sharon may see him as a Pioneer, but I'll keep my eyes on his good qualities—like the thoughtful way he's offering everyone white wine.*

At my turn, I said, "Thanks, but I only drink red. It doesn't turn to sugar in the body."

He nodded. "You've mentioned that before."

Sharon jabbed me with her eyes. Then she guzzled her first glass of white.

For the next few hours, I understood what a recovering alcoholic in a bar must feel, remaining sober while the surrounding gang got giddy. I was glad I brought along some short stories by Hemingway, so he could carry me into other worlds he created, until we landed in his old stomping grounds.

Fortunately, a sober driver named Jack Griffin was waiting for us at the tiny Ketchem airstrip. Jack looked in his 60s, yet he tossed our bags into the back of his van with the strength of a much younger man.

It felt like a sauna in his old van so we opened the windows. Making a sharp turn onto a two-lane road, Jack shouted, "Want air conditioning?"

After our unanimous, YES, Jack stepped on the gas. "Air conditioning," he said. His mischievous cackle blended with the high-speed breeze.

Several miles down the road, JOURNEYMAN pointed toward a sanctuary of trees at the base of a mountain and asked Jack to stop at the Hemingway memorial. There we gathered on a shaded bank above a glistening stream.

"I see how he recharged in all this beauty," I said.

"Until he blew his brains out," Jack said.

JOURNEYMAN patted my shoulder. "How many great writers have lived your cheerful life?"

"I write my way out of pain," I said.

JOURNEYMAN nodded and said we could still make it to happy hour at a Friday night hotspot. Then he shifted his attention to Sharon, Max and *the giddy gal pals*.

Walking back to the van with Jack, I said, "That was a quick stop."

"We need a constant change of scenery. A-D-D," he said.

"Interesting." Calling *Shotgun*, I had a front-row seat during Jack's narrated tour of Ketchem's scenic and celebrity hot spots, while JOURNEYMAN bantered with the others.

Has he been intimate with all of us? That made me queasy, as it had the night I left without getting involved with his friend, and Sharon's earlier ex—ARTISTOFLUV. It gave me an idea:

Hearts become revolving doors. Bodies playgrounds to explore. Hot young girls will earn encores. Chasing Love Matadors. *Hmm. That was cold. And hopefully unjustified.*

As Jack drove up to a three-cabin compound with mountains growing out of the back yard, he asked the question that was on my mind. "Who sleeps where?"

JOURNEYMAN said, "I assigned cabin mates on the plane before you got there, Hadley. So you're stuck with the bedroom next to mine."

Sharon gave me another visual jab before she and Max headed to their cabin the furthest away from mine. Stiff glances from *the girls* made me feel like I'd won some kind of competition. JOURNEYMAN wisely stayed back at the van with Jack.

We were given fifteen minutes to get settled and return to the van. Everyone gathered on time, except JOURNEYMAN. So Jack drove off without him and dropped us off in front of The Pioneer Saloon.

As we walked under their signpost, Sharon said, "Know why our Pioneer didn't show up? Too much unfinished pleasure to finish up."

She might be right. "Would you say that to his face?"

"I did, and he didn't deny it," Sharon said. "You're a bonder. So beware."

I followed Sharon, Max and *the girls* up to the massive wooden bar and felt the Pioneers watching us—the way a pack of coyotes eyeballed approaching bunnies. I sent out my *leave me alone vibe*. Thankfully, the Pioneers complied.

When I watched a muscled cowboy named Brian get cozy with Max, I whispered, "Aren't you back with Mark?"

"Not this weekend," Max said. She actually giggled while Brian steered her to his table with his hand in her back pocket.

I remembered my big chance to get back with Walter. While he'd been involved with Tina for six months, I'd often lose myself in fantasy—of a love never meant to be. Although I never acted on that fantasy, it still distracted me from intimate moments with my husband when he briefly moved back home:

> **It's not your hands I'm holding tight**
> **It's not your dreams I bear tonight**
> **It's not your heat that I desire**
> **I'm in your arms, but I feel his fire... The Boy You**
> **   Used To Be**

If I'd kept my eyes on Walter, instead of a pale imitation—could I have kept us together? I felt someone squeeze in next to me at the bar.

"I thought you'd be a happy drunk," Jack said.

"I'm thinking, not drinking."

"We can fix that. You've been summoned."

During our drive on curvy roads, Jack said, "You passed your first test, when you didn't throw a fit that you had to fly solo tonight. You're good for him, like he said."

"He confides in you."

Jack nodded. "He'll need a fiancé eventually, so hang in there."

"During his Pioneer phase?" I asked.

"Taking arrows in his back," Jack said, with a sigh that sounded like envy. "Yeah. He'll get sick of that. I hope you'll clear a safe landing for him."

I will not love a Pioneer, but we can still have fun at a jazz club, I thought as Jack dropped me off at the entrance to the sprawling Sun Valley Lodge. *I think Jack said, "Te Adorro." He adores you? I adore you? You're adorable?* I fiddled with a translation while I watched him rumble away, needing a new muffler for his old van.

Strolling into the Lodge, I followed the sound of smooth jazz piano and studied the photo wall of famous guests who'd partied or performed there in the last century.

Inside the Duchin room, a voluptuous pianist was casting her spell on a silver-haired crowd, including JOURNEYMAN at his front-row table.

Standing like a gentleman when I tiptoed up, he pulled my chair closer, "Count Basie played that piano. Frank sang here often. I thought you'd like it here."

Settling close to him, I noticed his martini and the bottle of red he'd let breathe for me. "You were confident," I teased.

"We like each other," he said, and we drank to that.

Do I apologize for my Solange thing? Or would it spoil things now? "Sorry about my meltdown over—"

He interrupted me, "Nobody's perfect. We all make mistakes."

"No mistakes. Only choices with love lessons attached like a bow," I said.

He squeezed my hand, "Most of us call them mistakes."

Holding hands as we listened to *easy lovin jazz,* I felt an *easy Ahhh* in his presence, as if we'd known each other for years. Leaning closer, I said, "I'm glad we can be together without any pressure for romance."

Nodding, he patted my hand. "Are you seeing anyone?"

"I was seeing a younger man who kept talking forever when he wasn't divorced yet. I didn't know what to believe."

"His first divorce?" JOURNEYMAN asked.

I nodded. He said, "It's capture mode. Typical when we're scared to be alone and even more scared to admit it. Second divorce is easier."

Those were big revelations. I pursued the one that concerned me the most. "You were married twice?"

He raised three fingers. "I believe in marriage, not monogamy."

"What about hot monogamy? Could that make you faithful forever?" I asked.

He chuckled. "Maybe. Now that forever's getting shorter."

"Reason to enjoy the now," I said. And we drank to that.

When I finished my first glass of red, I stifled a yawn. He suggested we make it an early night before I conked out right there.

"I made up for that the next morning, remember?"

He grinned, as if he also had fond memories of our *dawn of love*. Then he finished his drink and stood up. We left most of my bottle of French red for the servers to enjoy later, and he slid a twenty into the pianist's tip jar.

I saw her wink at him. I also noticed a few business cards mingling with her tips and wondered if he'd added his card to the mix. *He's a free agent*, I reminded myself as we slipped out in the middle of a familiar 40's tune, *At Last*.

During our drive home, Jack told us how he'd made the cover of the New York Post on his wedding day, when his bride-to-be visited him in jail, wearing her wedding gown to bail him out for speeding a hundred miles over the limit.

"She got me to the church on time," Jack said. Then he looked back at us. "I'll do the same for you."

"I don't have a girlfriend," JOURNEYMAN said.

That was the first I actually saw a restless glint in his eyes.

Ever the gentleman, JOURNEYMAN walked me to my room in our log cabin (not the Abe Lincoln kind, but the Ralph Lauren kind, ruggedly elegant). He hesitated outside my doorway. I asked him to wait right there.

I rushed to my suitcase and returned with wrapped gifts of my CD and my film, for his amusement in case he couldn't sleep, and I thanked him for a great day. With a smile, I tapped my door closed. A few seconds later, I heard him do the same to his.

Ahhh. Sweet exhaustion. I twirled around in a shower, slipped into a cotton gown and dove into my twin bed. I'd almost drifted to sleep when I heard three loud knocks and my door creaked open.

Jumping out of bed, I saw JOURNEYMAN wearing a cotton robe and a shy grin.

"I can hear the creek from my room," he said. "It's not fair of me, not to share it with you."

When he made me laugh, I threw my arms around him, and we tangoed into his room.

His endearing foreplay freed me to be a light-hearted lover that night. No worries about outcome or others who might be waiting in the wings. Only joy with this man in this moment. Joy that lingered, while I rested my head on his chest, hearing his heartbeat blend with the sound of our creek. Joy that inspired me:

> **Let's be light-hearted lovers. Let's be intimate friends.**
> **Let love bring us together. Let's be Free Again.**
> **Light-hearted lovers are one in the now**
> **Caring, not duty, our only vow...**

Could I live up to those lyrics? I wondered as I drifted into a delicious sleep.

The sun tickled my eyelids and woke me early. I felt at home beside him, watching him sleep. He may have felt my gaze as he started to smile.

Gently, I traced his dimple and whispered, "Maybe it's this simple. Sharing the sounds of the creek."

He swatted my bottom, "Get ready for a marathon bike ride."

That felt like a brush off, but I was more concerned about something else. "It's my back's first road test, so I'll do my best."

"That's the spirit," he said.

A half-hour later, our jock-chic gang gathered at a row of mountain bikes on our gravel drive. A gallant host, JOURNEYMAN knelt down to adjust the seat height for each of his guests, rewarded with a glimpse of their tanned legs in the process.

During that preparation lull, *the girls* announced the names of their lucky pioneers from last night. When Max spoke up, adding Brian's name to the list, I suspected her reconciliation with Mark was in jeopardy.

At Sharon's turn, she didn't mention a pioneer. In a suspicious tone, she asked what had happened to me last night.

I saw JOURNEYMAN look up at me. "I went to bed early," I said. Then he nodded his approval.

"You need beauty sleep to look good. Like my mom," said Jennifer. When the grownups groaned, she squealed, "She hasn't faked her face."

"Or anything else," said Alison, cupping her fake breasts in her hands, as if comparing two big melons. "Why not improve mother nature?"

"Do they feel real?" Sharon asked, and Alison let her take a squeeze. Sharon raised her eyebrows and nodded, clearly impressed. Alison offered me a feel, and I passed politely, although repelled by the notion of carving bodies for beauty.

Then Alison offered her chest and a come-to-me smile to JOURNEY-MAN, asking if he wanted *another turn*. I looked to him for confirmation of what I'd already suspected.

He kept a poker face as he said, "I'll give my turn to Jack."

"My turn for what?" Jack appeared out of the morning mist, riding his bike up to us. But the moment had passed.

JOURNEYMAN asked Jack to adjust Alison's bike, then he gave me a quick glance. I could've said a guilty glance, but why put a negative spin on it?

As Jack adjusted my bike next, he said I had *gorgeous gams*. I thanked him, aware how that term had dated him.

JOURNEYMAN rode down the gravel drive and set the pace for us to follow. I pedaled gently at first, to see if my back could handle it. Glancing back at Jack, I said, "Did he ask you to stick with me?"

He grinned, "A sweet assignment."

A mile or so into an uphill climb, the gang waited for us to catch up before they turned off road. "The jungle short cut," I moaned, as my bike wobbled over thick brush, with Jack trailing close behind me.

"Another test," Jack said.

I shrugged, feeling relieved my back was letting me stay in the game. A minute later, I saw JOURNEYMAN look back at me, as if checking whether I'd passed his test. Nodding, he circled back toward the pavement for a smooth ride.

We stopped for fuel at a bakery in town. As many of the locals started wishing Jack a happy birthday, JOURNEYMAN seemed surprised and suggested he invite some friends over for a barbeque at the cabins that night.

By the time we finished our muffins and coffees outside, Jack had invited a dozen passers-by to his party and JOURNEYMAN had called his caterers.

While getting back on our bikes, Sharon asked Jack how old he was today. "Your age. If today's seventy is yesterday's fifty," he said, serving up another cackle.

Ahhh. His joyful spirit extended the warranty on his chassis.

Riding at the back of the pack, we followed JOURNEYMAN through town and into a car dealership, where he stopped beside a silver hybrid—wrapped in a big red bow.

"Happy Birthday," he said.

As Jack beheld his new Prius, we applauded and cheered. Gulping down a wave of emotion, Jack was speechless and nodded his thanks to JOURNEYMAN, who suggested we bike over to Fox Creek Trail for a hike.

Jack must've heard me sigh, because he asked if I'd like to go on his virgin voyage. I hopped in, while he tossed our bikes in the back. The inside temp could've baked a turkey, so Jack blasted real air conditioning and smiled when it cooled in a flash.

The new-car fumes didn't seem to bother him, but I opened my window and stuck my head outside. "The smell makes my throat swell."

"Your throat. Your back. What's next?" Jack asked.

"I've always been healthy," I said.

"Before mid-life meltdown. Sneaky bastard. Takes guts to get to my age."

"Neither of my parents did," I said. "They barely got past my age now."

He gave me a long glance. "Then grab it now, while you can."

"Doesn't that thinking start up short marriages, and break up long ones?"

Turning onto my gravel drive, Jack said, "Smart cookie." Then he dropped me off at my doorstep and sped off.

I was glad to grab some solitude, a lazy afternoon of reading and dozing on a shaded Adirondack chair. When I heard some motion in the creek,

I peeked around the corner of the front porch to see what was happening. With storm clouds closing in on this summer afternoon, my entire world telescoped to the vision of one man.

My dear pioneer was standing knee-deep in our creek, wearing hip boots and casting for whatever fly-fishermen tried to catch. Keeping my quiet distance, I admired his rhythm, calm and grace in the moving water, thinking *I want him to catch me.*

With a contented smile, I settled down with another Hemingway story. Fifteen pages later, the rain came and JOURNEYMAN returned empty handed.

"Hey, fisherman," I said.

He grinned. "You didn't interrupt me out there. Thanks."

"If you wanted company, you would've said something."

"Girls don't get it. They don't need *toes up time* like we do."

"That usually turned into *toes down time* with Walter."

He scrunched up his face. "Walter was younger in those days. See you after my nap." He opened the screen door and hesitated, "We could fit in a gallery opening before dinner at eight."

"Sounds great," I said, my thoughts revving up. *He's amazing. We like the same things. I love being with him. Whoa...* I went inside to change.

Luckily, I'd packed a couple cocktail dresses, since I couldn't zip the first one over my swollen belly. *Odd, since I hadn't been eating carbs or sugar. Oh well.*

We all were dressed to thrill when we sauntered into a gallery to see a new sculpture exhibit. I noticed that JOURNEYMAN stayed a few steps behind us. At a fork in the gallery flow, when our gal pals headed right, he headed left and merged into another well-dressed crowd.

Sharon caught me watching him. "Scottie's seeing someone who works here, so he won't be seen with us," she said.

Casually, I shifted my gaze to the painted-bronze curves of a long-haired waif, whose rail-thin legs embraced the back of her neck in a yoga pose. "Got evidence?" I asked.

"He told me, during our bike ride. He said he was meeting so many wonderful women, but nobody turned him on like the one he wanted most."

"Who's the lucky woman?" I asked, thinking it might be me.

She shrugged. "His kids and friends don't like her. So he might move to an island to be alone with her. He's hooked, even though she makes him crazy."

I thought of Solange, and my chest tightened. *Stop thinking. Start drinking. Merlot stays. Pioneer goes.* I tugged on the waiter's tux and plucked a glass of red from his tray. "Serenity is sexy," I said.

The waiter shrugged. Sharon and I drank to that. We drank to a lot of toasts during Jack's birthday bash that night, while I steered clear of my pioneer. I was surprised he played the DVD of my short film on our flat-screen TV for forty guests to watch me Tango with a 20 year-old fantasy lover named *Ernesto—*

I stood in the background, watching reactions. Luckily, the film gave the gang a few laughs, as intended. And *my love, Merlot,* helped me find something to laugh about with each guest—except for one young girl, who was snuggling on the lap of a grandfather figure on the same chaise where I'd been reading that afternoon.

I stifled a gasp. Jack said, "It's a living. Trading youth for golden pre-nups."

Too tipsy to think of a polite reply, I kept my thoughts to myself:

> **She stakes her claim to pre-nup deals**
> **Delivers heirs, her fortune's sealed**
> **Her new career trades youth for gold**
> **Her catch believes she loves him old**

That kind of thinking, combined with my forth glass of red, made the room start to spin. I tried to stay on my feet while I snuck into my room. Before birthday cake. Before the swirling moon outside my window made me sick, I threw off my clothes and conked out.

My bedside clock flashed 4:10 when I opened my eyes and wished I hadn't. *Whoa. Whoa. Woke up in a Merlot haze. My my my head and my belly aches.*

I rose above my dizziness when I got out of bed and wrote that down, along with the lines I remembered from *Love Matadors*. *If I felt cozy here, I wouldn't write this stuff.* Sliding into bed, I moaned myself back to sleep. When I opened my eyes again after ten, I noticed my bike was parked alone on the gravel drive. *Thankfully, I can recover in quiet.* I soothed my aching head in a lazy shower.

Then I burnt some toast, and JOURNEYMAN walked in during my first bite. "You're quite the cook," he said.

"It soaks up alcohol like charcoal," I said, hoping the toast would stay down.

While pouring a big bowl of cheerios, he said, "I knocked last night, but you were out cold. You missed some fun."

"I had too much fun." He held his spoon like a shovel as he dug in. *He's adorable without trying,* I thought.

"You're a funny drunk," he said. "That's a plus."

"I'm done drinking," I said, more than half serious.

Between munches, he said, "I'll be depressed when you leave today."

"You're not flying back with us?"

Looking down, he said, "I'm staying here 'til I go to Australia next week."

"Are you bringing a date?"

He threw his head back in laughter. "That's like bringing a biscuit to a banquet. I know my limitations, so I'm bringing Jack as my birddog."

It felt like a punch in my gut. "That was mean," I said.

"Honest. It's only fair to let you know where we stand."

That works both ways, Buster. "There's always a greener trail, a better catch, someone sexier—newer," I said. "So happy trails, my dear Pioneer."

He swallowed hard. "Why can't I say, NO?"

His confused eyes softened me. "Because YES is more fun. And you like *diving in* more than a long swim. Right now."

"I always leave," he said, gently. "I don't want to hurt you."

"I won't let you." I gulped down some disappointment, but some escaped. "So we lost our chance?" He pursed his lips and looked down, without saying a word.

"Do you agree it's time to move on?" I asked. His silence was my answer. I went to my room and got ready to leave. A half hour later, I wheeled my bag toward Jack's new SUV and saw JOURNEYMAN, standing knee-deep in our creek, casting his line. I felt it tug at my heart. *How long will I feel connected to him?* I wondered as we drove off.

12. A SONGBIRD'S CALL

I wanted a peaceful flight home, so I sat alone by a back-row window, cuddling a pillow and blanket. During take-off, *the girls* removed their *party-girl personas*.

Jennifer started the unveiling in a spiteful tone. "I decided to spend every dime on divorce lawyers rather than give it to Barry and his bimbo."

"That's how you chop off his dick and serve it as appetizers—legally," Alison said. "I also had to sue Eddie for a hundred grand for my back surgery."

"No health insurance?" Max asked her.

Alison's eyes bulged as she said, "I got screwed by my new insurance which wouldn't pay for treatment I started before divorce—that's when Eddie threw me against the wall and broke a few bones."

"She threw a chair at him first. So you can't totally blame him," Jennifer said.

Alison sent her a steely glare. "Whose friend are you?"

Jennifer apologized, and the rest of us sat there in silence. Shaking her head, Sharon said, "Violence is the only legitimate reason to break up a family."

"What about a lack of kindness? That's why I'm divorcing Mark, for sure this time," Max said.

"Kindness can be taught. It's a learned behavior," I said.

Alison leaned toward Max and announced, "It's revenge time. You absolutely can't let him see your kids."

Jennifer let out a devilish, "*Yeah*," which gave me chills of concern for their ruptured families. I expected Max to tell them she didn't have any kids, but she didn't bother.

In her extra-calm voice Max said, "Would you ladies yield the floor to my favorite songwriter who found another way to say *Good-bye*."

An elegant segue, I thought, as all eyes turned to me. "I don't like to remember this, but I felt your awful anger when my husband left me. I found the path out of it, thanks to an unexpected guide." I intended to share my song until they stopped me—

> I was asking *Why Me* sipping my tea
> When a wing*ed messenger answered me
> A songbird crashed into my patio door
> Changing my life as she fell to the floor
>
> I knelt by her side, looked in her eyes
> Her gift was a song that mesmerized
> As her last breaths echoed in my ear
> Her glorious message was crystal clear
>
> She said *Good-Bye* in a burst of beauty—Songbird
> She let go of life with a song that renewed me—
>   Songbird
> She left here doing what she was born to do best
> Guiding me through my most challenging test—
>   Songbird
> She sang— (Whistle Songbird's Call)
>
> When I looked at my losses, I felt like hell
> When I looked at what's left, I could tell
> My songbird showed me the path out of pain
> My songbird showed me how to live again
>
> Filled with rage and regret that my old life would die
> I'd like to learn from her song, how to say Good-Bye
> I'll let go of lost love by creating beauty
> As thanks to my guide for her song that renewed
>   me— (Whistle *Songbird's Call*)

Alison shrieked, "Screw that. We'd end up as friends."

"Never," Jennifer said. Then she high-fived Jennifer, as if partners in crime.

Their silent girlfriend, a shy brunette named Molly, turned to me. She patted her chest—growing in stature in my eyes. I nodded, thinking, *She got it.* I could only wish she'd be a voice of harmony for *the girls.* I couldn't wait to get away from their angry energy when we landed in Chicago.

While waiting near the belly of the jet for our luggage to be unloaded, Sharon invited me to her house with Max for a rooftop picnic during fireworks. I felt uneasy. I'd kept my distance, knowing she'd be upset if she found out about JOURNEYMAN and me. I knew I wasn't treating her right, and I wanted to change that.

"We need to talk about our Pioneer," I said.

Sharon tensed up and looked away. Max said, "Next topic. The fireworks I want to see start at dark."

Sharon turned to me. "It was one night of good sex, two days of good sports and a free ride on his jet."

"One way to look at it," I said, tactfully. Her crude view of my connection with JOURNEYMAN wasn't what upset me most. "He should've let me tell you."

"Tell me what?" Sharon asked.

"Holy shit," Max shrieked. She'd connected the dots a beat ahead of us.

I felt clobbered. Sharon seemed too stunned to speak. Max's voice rose an octave, "What about the *no best friends rule,* in effect since high school?"

"Our Alpha Pioneer," Sharon sighed, as if laughing it off. "Didn't I warn you, Hadley?"

"Now I need magnifiers when I see men. It's not any easier—coming of age again. Sorry for the rhyme."

"Lyrics flow when you're feeling low," Max said.

"Let's delete him with our love, Merlot." Sharon finished that verse.

With a crack of thunder, the dark skies opened up and gave me an acceptable excuse to ask for a rain check. Sharon and Max shared a cab downtown, while I drove home alone.

I was trying to see the taillights ahead of me through sheets of rain. In a flash of lightning, I saw JOURNEYMAN's sneaky grin.

When my cell rang, I said, "JOURNEYMAN?"

As soon as I heard, "I missed you," I knew I had to cover up my mistake.

"Are you back from your journey, PETLOVR?"

"Did you miss me?" he asked.

I slowly pulled around a stalled car in the center lane of I-55 and told him the truth. "I don't let myself miss anyone, anymore. But if I did, I might've missed you."

"I stopped by your house and called to see if you needed a backup generator."

"What happened?"

"Power's been out for days.

"I didn't know. I've been away with friends," I said.

"Platonic?"

The thought of lying made me cringe. So I was vague. "Our private lives are best kept private, unless we're a couple."

He took a deep breath and sighed, "You couldn't wait for me, Hadley?"

His sad tone triggered my regret. "We should talk."

"Nothing more to say."

When PETLOVR hung up on me, he made me feel like a pioneer. I pounded my steering wheel and cried, "DAMN."

Thunder rolled, like my angry echo.

13. MID-LIFE MELTDOWN

When I walked into my dark house, the security system was beeping to tell me what PETLOVR had just told me. I bypassed the beeping. Then I groped my way into my Dining room, lit a candle and went straight to bed without washing my face. I let the thunderous symphony soothe me into sleep.

The smell of our creek woke me when it was still dark. *A dream of my fisherman?* A sinking feeling reminded me he'd moved on. When the fishy scent lingered, I lit my candle and tracked down its source to the basement, where each footstep on the gym rug sloshed up disgusting water.

In the utility closet, I glanced at the splattered walls and a mound of mud near the sump pump and its backup battery, and figured they'd fought to their deaths.

I hurried upstairs to call my insurance broker, Rebecca, and realized my portable phone also died. Fortunately, my only landline transcended its decorative use and let me leave a voicemail for my broker.

"My back-up generator could've used a backup," I said. Then I heard a steady *drip drip drip,* and aimed my candlelight at my cathedral ceiling where rain was falling in a dozen spots. "My whole house is having a meltdown," I cried. "Call me, Rebecca."

My grandfather clock was chiming eight times when she returned my call. "You paid top dollar for a masterpiece policy. We'll handle everything, Hadley."

I was skeptical. When a three-man crew arrived an hour later, I breathed easier. When they started *demolition* wearing oxygen masks, I expressed my concern to Ian, the 30ish captain. His response sounded hollow in his mask.

"Mold grows fast in this weather," he said. "Stay in a hotel and go shopping for a few days, while I make things safe for humans."

Shopping isn't my calm in chaos. I set up a canvas and paints in my patio, so Ian could reach me, as needed. On the bright side, I finally made time for the portrait I'd wanted to paint all summer. From a small photo, I painted a large portrait of Lily, resting near me—the way I liked to remember her.

The sun had been down for an hour when I started painting her sweet, folded under paw and I was startled by a question—

"Think she's still got influence?" a familiar voice asked from his distant view of Lily.

"PETLOVR." I took off my readers before I swiveled to face him. The weight on his shoulders visibly dragged him down.

"Sorry I hung up on you, but—" He cleared his throat and looked into my eyes. "I think I could forget all this and be a couple again. If you're still available."

Hmm. I see how I've hurt him, but he gave me a pass. Why don't I trust it? "What about your trophy wife?" I asked.

He straightened up like a professor starting a lecture. "According to my online dictionary, a trophy wife is a much younger woman whom a man shows off like a prize. So I'm right. You can never be my trophy. And that's not what I want anyway."

I turned toward my canvas and said, "You've cleared that up."

"Don't turn away. You'll want to hear this," he said.

Curious to see how he'd weasel his way out of this one, I faced him.

"You're a Ferrari," he said. "Dangerous, requiring skill to handle, sometimes uncomfortable, but always more exciting than a silly trophy."

"True. Also from your online dictionary?" I teased. When he chuckled, I thought, *So what? Shows initiative. Stop being so critical.*

Slapping his forehead, he said, "I said you've got lines. I meant laugh lines."

I activated those lines with a grin. "I over-reacted."

Grabbing my waist with both hands, he drew me closer and said in his sexy growl, "You're a hot—momma."

I felt guarded, but I was more concerned about the hurt look in his eyes. "You've corrected your mistakes. A-plus for effort," I said.

He threw up his hands. "You act like I've got to pass a test before we're a couple, and that's bullshit. When does unconditional love kick in?"

My throat tightened at my thought, *The noose isn't loose.* I told him, "It doesn't. I moved on."

"You'd run from real love?" he asked.

"From a hustler. You never stop," I said. He raised his brow like a bow, so I expected his sharp tone.

"Now I see what Walter did. He made you hard. Love is soft," he said.

I snapped, "I never ran from Walter."

"He ran from you. Now you diss a great guy, who'll stand by you no matter what. Did you ever think I might be your last chance? My new dating coach said you'd be as hard to place as a ten-year old orphan."

That took my breath away, but he didn't seem to notice as he continued, "You should be grateful I want to love you, at your—"

I stifled his blundering lips with my fingertips. "You're a jerk," I said, but not in anger. It was an elated AHA—because I finally realized what my body was telling me all along. "You've made it easy to say, *NEXT*."

Shaking his head, he said, "You want transparency—then you twist what I say, so you can chase another notch on your belt. I feel sorry for you. I do."

As he marched down the aisle of my tropical garden, I tried not to shoot him in the back, but I couldn't resist. "You couldn't make your wife love you either," I shouted. My fingers flew to my lips. I hated to end things on a mean note, but he deserved it.

In my quiet lull before sleep that night, I realized my children and I were staying in the same hotel where SPIRITRIDER had stayed—when he'd traveled 2000 miles for me to make his ears wriggle. I'd failed that test. I'd passed a few of JOURNEYMAN's tests. I gave him an F for his wanderlust.

PETLOVR had balked at dating tests. Yet he'd wanted unconditional love from someone he'd just met. Isn't that the toughest test of all?

I plumped my king-size pillow in the king-sized bed I shared with Jade, who said, "You're frowning, Mom."

"I'm thinking," I said. Then I opened my eyes, "I stopped seeing Doctor Mitchell because he drained my enthusiasm."

"Why can't you just have fun?" Jade asked.

"Good question," I muttered.

In the flickering light of Letterman on TV, Logan said, "I never met the guy."

I sat up in my bed and told him, "He wanted to play hockey with you, but—"

"He plays hockey, piano, and he's a doctor?" Logan asked.

"And he still looks good," Jade added.

"I hope you know what you're doing, Moot," Logan said.

"I do what's best for me and you two. It feels right," I said.

"We'll both be away. So do what's best for you," Logan said. He clicked off the TV and settled into sleep, unaware that his earlier comment had affected me like a jolt of caffeine.

What am I doing? Well. I won't bond with the wrong guy. Things felt right with their dad from the start—so I wove my thoughts, feelings and actions into our tapestry. And I'm glad I did. Except it made the unraveling too painful. It still hurts to think about it. I've got to remember the love.

I looked at my sleeping children and let my mind be lulled by their breathing. Then I stroked my cheek, ever so gently—the way their dad used to ease me into sleep. *Love leaves traces…*

So does construction. During the two weeks it took Ian to get my house back in shape, the nasty construction smells often made my throat swell. I refused to circulate those fumes through my air conditioning vents, so they lingered in the thick July heat, like bitter perfume in a steamy church service.

Ian brought in several fans to make things bearable for his team and mine. I thanked him with a big tip, on the day he finished my home repairs.

The next day I flew to see Doctor G, so he could finish my back repairs. To celebrate (and test) the success of his third and final round of injections, Doctor G joined me for a round of golf, as we'd planned a month earlier, when JOURNEYMAN was still in the picture. *His loss.*

Whenever Doctor G was my guest for golf, we preferred to walk my hilly desert course while playing the game. I felt confident I could walk and swing lightly, so I carried four clubs in my featherweight *Sunday Bag*, and enjoyed pain-free play.

With an easy swing, I made a 190-hard drive on a par 5, and Doctor G called me *his swinging testimonial for treating disc disease*.

"So that's what knocked me to my knees with a sneeze," I said, playfully.

"It's not that simple," he said, casually. I didn't give it much thought.

I may have four-putt the 9th hole because I was distracted by the smell of smoke from a controlled burn in the mountains near Los Alamos forty miles away. It was having the same affect on me as Ian's construction fumes.

I mentioned this to Doctor G—of course I waited until he sunk a 15-foot putt and we hustled off the 9th green so a foursome could chip on.

Doctor G set his clubs on a grassy bank near the clubhouse. He tapped my neck with his fingertips, like notes on a trumpet.

I complained, "The noose isn't loose."

"Let's see what's behind that pain in your neck," Doctor G said.

I blurted the answer. "My sexual healing was too stressful, so I gave it up."

As we walked up the path toward the sprawling adobe clubhouse, he said, "That doesn't begin until you're in a committed relationship, with deep intimacy and no secrets, for at least four years."

"By four weeks, things get too complicated for me," I said.

We sat down at an outdoor bar with views of a pastel sunset over extinct volcanoes. Then he sighed, "I'm afraid that's why our friends in lasting relationships seem to be outliving us single folks."

"I don't want to hear that," I said. Hmm. *If settlers outlive pioneers, then—*

The college-age waiter took our order of two draft beers and buffalo burgers. When he walked away, I said, "Do you think we should choose a good match with good values and then learn to love them, in spite of their quirks?"

"That sounds good." Doctor G rubbed his mouth, as if hiding a grin.

"But does it work?" I asked.

He rolled his eyes. "Not if you ask my ex wives."

Lopping up olive oil with warm bread, I said, "That's because you choose challenging mates. I'm holding out for someone like me."

"If you're both the same, one is unnecessary," he said.

"I meant full of contentment instead of challenges."

"Get another yellow dog. No sparks, no fire," he said.

The waiter brought our beers, and we clicked glasses without naming a toast.

I pursued my point. "Starting a new life's hard enough. Why choose someone who makes it harder?"

"Attraction isn't a choice," Doctor G said. "Unconscious beliefs and cellular memories drive us to choose a date or a mate. They also trigger disease. Until you flip your cellular switch from stress to healing mode, I can't help you. You're wasting money on treatments 'til you flip that switch."

"I'm terrified of a negative thought," I cried.

"That's a negative thought," he said. "Most of the world is emotionally negative and can't be helped by positive thinking. Taking positive action is what's needed to rewire the brain."

"You told me this. I do this. But something's dragging me down," I said.

He prescribed *the secret weapon* that had worked for me before. When he reminded me what it was, I breathed easier. I'd used it during my long bout of grief over lost love. I used it again the next day during a Health-Kinesiology session with Nonnie.

While I relaxed on Nonnie's treatment table, she taped batteries—slim glass vials containing squiggly wire sculptures—to my crown, my forehead and throat, and between my breasts. While propping the 5th battery against my jeans at my public bone, she said, "This one revives sexual energy."

"How?" I asked.

"Do you need to know how a TV works to enjoy the show?"

"If JOURNEYMAN saw these batteries, he'd call us both *kooks*," I said.

"Tell him Einstein proved everything in the universe is made of energy. Energetic beings need energetic healing."

"I don't tell him anything. He moved on."

"Too many Solanges in the world," Nonnie said. "Feel the frustration and let these babies zap it."

The frustration felt like pressure in my throat. After a few minutes it passed. That pattern was repeated each time Nonnie asked me to feel a sore spot: fear of trusting, fear of abandonment and betrayal, fear of being alone. Somehow the batteries turned an *ouch* into an *ahhh*. I left there an hour later relaxed and ready for a nap.

I conked out during my naked sunbathing session on my roof deck, and a mysterious sensation woke me. I felt Lily chomping on my beach towel, like she was pulling me away from the stairs in a tug of war. My head was rattling on the planks. When I opened my eyes, my hair was standing on end, as if a lightning bolt were striking and wouldn't stop.

"Whooooooooooaaaa." My sigh rumbled like a scream on buffalo-thunder. *Am I dreaming?*

A few seconds later, my head jolted to a stop. Though I never saw Lily, I felt her leave. I held my very sore neck and slowly rolled my head toward the stairs, where I saw two furry kittens, eyeing me, while another kitten and their very big mama followed them upstairs.

I didn't know if they were mountain lions or bobcats, but I knew I had to get away fast. I grabbed my towel and tossed my cell phone at the kittens, distracting them. Then I hopped onto my guardrail, slid down a slope onto my flat roof, and scooted into a hug with my delicate aspen tree, which bent down and cushioned my thud onto tufts of buffalo grass. *Nothing's broken. I'm strong.*

From the safety of my kitchen, I watched big mama tending to her kittens on my roof deck above my guest casita. A wildlife rescue team arrived a couple hours later to take these houseguests to a new home.

Manuel, the team spokesperson, told me the mama bobcat had birthed her babies on my roof deck this summer. "Why would wild animals settle in my tame neighborhood?"

"For water in a drought," he said. "You water buffalo grass, which feeds bunnies, who feed coyotes, mountain lions and bobcats. It's the wild west."

Watching their van drive away, it occurred to me that we're all seeking water in a drought in some way. When we find what quenches our parched soul, we settle down.

When I saw Doctor G that afternoon, my neck was visibly swollen. There was a sense of urgency in his muscle testing. He said my liver was loaded with toxins like a pitcher overflowing its rim. He gave me a *liquid acupuncture push*—dozens of rapid-fire injections into my neck, lymph glands, liver and legs and feet.

"You've been poisoned, and we have to find the cause," Doctor G said.

I was stunned, vaguely aware of his ongoing testing. It ended when he held up a vial and told me that my body's struggling to get rid of a pesticide that was outlawed decades ago. He concluded, "Your ex didn't poison you, but something in your childhood did."

"Walter would never poison me," I said.

Doctor G asked if I were a farm girl or if I drank bug killer as a kid.

I almost laughed, but I saw he was serious. "Our home was built on former farmland."

"Often contaminated with chemicals," he said.

A childhood picture popped into my mind, and I told him how we used to play baseball on our street most summer nights. Whenever the magic fogging truck passed by, we'd run behind it, laughing while we were hidden in its stinky fog.

As I watched him shake his head, I felt betrayed by the adults in charge. "Nobody tried to stop us in those days," I said.

"It's worse now, when thousands of man-made poisons are making us sick," he said. "There are safe, natural alternatives for each one of them. So why use cannons to kill mosquitoes?" he asked. "First of all—"

I saw fire in his eyes, but I had to interrupt him. At five bucks a minute for his time, his passionate views would be too costly. "We can't change that. How can we change this?"

He said other toxins also had to go. He recommended several treatments each week for a few months to get the job done faster than home dosing. I chose the latter, so I could be at home with Jade. Then he asked me to stick around until things stabilized, to make sure I didn't end up in the E-R with anaphalactic shock.

That didn't sound good. Plus I felt weak. So I stayed and became his pincushion. A wise choice, since my neck kept swelling up, and his treatments kept bringing it down.

Fortunately, I felt better after every treatment. So I was able to go on a hike and enjoy several meals with the tribe, two more H-K sessions with Nonnie, and I also started making notes for my novel, thinking I'd get around to writing it someday.

While I flew home after two weeks of treatments, my spirits were soaring. I was grateful I'd bounced back from another health challenge with relative ease.

During that flight, things changed. I wouldn't be exaggerating if I said, "My world came crashing down."

14. THE ONE-TWO PUNCH

I've often wished I hadn't used the plane's rest room a half hour before we landed. When I flushed the toilette, I breathed a blast of chemical air that made my throat swell. I asked the flight attendant for water, and I swallowed five capsules that Doctor G had given me, *in case of an emergency*. The swelling stopped as we made our descent for landing. I felt a renewed sense of security while we taxied to the gate.

That changed when I reached into my overhead compartment and wished I hadn't. When I pulled out my very light roller bag, I felt something shift in my neck, like the earth plates during a quake. My bag tumbled out of my left hand. I froze in fear, or pain, I couldn't distinguish.

I did yoga breathing while passengers filed past me. When the aisle was clear, I wasn't sure I could walk. Each baby step brought tears to my eyes.

So did lying in the OPEN MRI tube for 45 minutes that afternoon, trying not to scream. So did the diagnosis that my neighbor-friends, Doctors Kabir and Meeka, gave me when they stopped by my house that night.

Kabir told me several neck discs had ruptured forward and compressed my spine, causing a break in the same spot as Christopher Reeve, the star of *Superman*.

Meeka said I was luckier, because I could walk and a neurosurgeon could fix it.

Kabir said there was a serious risk of paralysis before surgery, if I stumbled or if someone bumped me. "So you must be very still until surgery," he said. Meeka repeated that warning.

A long blink was my reply. They velcroed a soft brace around my neck to protect me from bumps, and I felt supported. It hurt to move my mouth, so I didn't speak.

I felt my bangs shaking on my forehead, while Kabir gave me the name of a top neurosurgeon who'd developed this new procedure. Then Meeka gave me samples of new pain pills and asked me to call them anytime I needed them. Their kindness brought tears to my eyes.

Although it hurt when I swallowed two pain pills, it hurt worse when my liver spit them out. So I never took another one. Every movement became a test I couldn't pass. I couldn't tolerate the pressure of a pillow on my neck, so lying in bed was impossible. I couldn't sleep unless I floated weightless in my tub. So I alternated two hours of *being still* at my desk, with two hours of floating in my tub, day and night, while I waited for surgery.

I also got my will in order—in case I couldn't survive the pain. It was a monster in a horror film, and I couldn't look away. I couldn't pick up anything with my left hand. Yet I found I could rest it on my computer keyboard and tap keys with my fingertips, so I could surf medical sites on the internet and work on my book.

Unable to lift an egg or a pan to boil it, at least I could dial my cell for carryout of any meals that Jade didn't offer to prepare. It was hard for her to see me like this.

"You're our rock. Our family doesn't work without you, Mom."

I assured her I'd be stronger than ever—after my surgery, and I desperately wanted to believe it.

I waited two weeks to see that top neurosurgeon. The day of my initial consultation, I sat for two hours in his waiting room outside his office in the hospital. Ten fragile patients hunched over in wheel chairs were waiting with me, so I felt blessed that I could take baby steps when the nurse called my name.

I greeted that top neurosurgeon by suggesting he provide internet access, music, TV and bottled water for his patients when he made us wait two hours to see him. He raised his brow as if surprised and grunted.

After a quick exam of my MRIs and me, he said I was a poster-child for his new procedure. He said that my injuries were notably severe without trauma. He explained how he'd rebuild my neck and mentioned a list of things that could go wrong during surgery, including paralysis.

Whoa. I asked to speak with a success story where it all went right. He told me he'd have a patient call me. Then he asked if I wanted to schedule surgery.

"If it includes morphine, book it," I said. He shook my hand, gently, and said he'd see me in two months. *Two months in the tub. I'll be a prune by then.*

A few days later, the neurosurgeon's *success story* called me. After she introduced herself, I said, "I hear pain in your voice."

"Not as bad as before surgery last year, but constant. At least I'm not paralyzed."

I thanked her for her honesty and wished her well. But I was devastated. If she were the success story, then surgery was my last resort. I had to find another solution.

I was in tears when I called Doctor G, asking for a second opinion. I explained my injury and said I was terrified of paralysis. He said he'd been working to avoid something like this, *but clearly not fast enough.* He said he could help me grow a new neck—bones, discs, everything—by giving my body all the nutrients needed to rebuild itself. He was confident he'd achieve same results on my neck as on my lower back.

I took my inner pulse, looking for signs of resistance. It felt like a hundred trillion cells were in agreement, so I made the biggest decision of my life, "I'll trust you, Doctor G."

That night I explained my decision to Jade and Logan (who joined us via conference call from his dorm room). I recapped my reasons for avoiding surgery and for choosing the treatment that had helped my lower back. They listened without commenting. I booked my flight for Albuquerque.

On the eve of my trip, Walter called me to say our children were worried about me. So he'd called Kabir, who told him I was being reckless. Walter asked, "Do you want to ruin Jade's senior year if you're paralyzed? Think long and hard before you make that trip, Hadley."

"I've thought of nothing else. There's no guarantee either way." In an emotional whisper, I told him what had been on my mind during recent sleepless nights. "I'm sorry for anything I did to hurt you, in case my karma caused this."

"Let it go. I have," Walter said. "I don't like to hear you in so much pain. None of us do. I hope you know what you're doing. For your sake and our children."

"Uh huh." I hung up as my tears welled up. Again. I'd read there were lots of healing chemicals in tears, so I let them flow—again—while *being still* and silent. That was my new hidden talent since my injury. *Could tears carve a path down my cheeks?*

The next morning, I took a taxi to Midway Airport. Because of my slow pace, I allowed two hours for boarding. I asked my neighbor in line at security to lift my shoes into a bin for screening. Then I was asked to go through an extra security check of my neck brace, on which I'd draped a colorful Matisse silk scarf.

Otherwise, I traveled lightly. Since I couldn't lift my wallet, all I carried with me was an envelope containing my MRIs; plus my pockets were filled with a photo ID, my boarding pass, car keys, a charge card and some cash.

I took one baby step at a time toward my gate. An older man driving a trolley offered me a lift. When I whispered my thanks, his kind smile prompted another rush of my tears.

During the flight, I stayed away from the toilette, knowing I couldn't tolerate another flush of chemical air. During my drive from the airport, I could barely turn toward the side-view mirror, so I stayed in the pokey lane. *Should I be driving myself? What else can I do?*

The 60-mile drive was smooth, until bumps in Santa Fe streets felt like double-edged blades jabbing my neck. My eyes were swollen into slits when I saw Doctor G. He gasped when he saw me. Silently, I gave him my MRIs, and he helped me onto his table, lying face down.

I couldn't stand another drop of pain, so I sobbed through a dozen injections of 20 CCs of nutrients in my neck. Afterwards, I saw his eyes were red and swollen, too.

"Hard for both of us," I said. He said it would get easier, and then he explained why.

I focused on the bright side that night, when my children called me for results of my first treatment. They reached me while I was floating in hot water. I told them the shots gave me my first glimpse of pain relief outside my tub—my sign that I was on the right path.

"I'd been upset I had to wait so long for surgery," I said. "Now I see it was a blessing."

Jade said, "We can't count all our blessings at once, because some are in disguise."

"Do wounds go to the wise, so we light a path for the other guys?" I asked.

"That's incentive to be stupid," Logan said. "When will your neck be fixed?"

I calmly reported highlights of what Doctor G had told me:

I'm overloaded with man-made toxins that wore away discs and bone, which were meant to stay strong for 100 years of hard labor in the field. The toxic force that broke my neck was like slamming head-on into a semi trailer on a mountain curve. It could take two years of de-toxing and re-building treatments to fix it.

After a long silence, Logan said, "Surgery would fix it in one day."

"That's my Plan B. But it doesn't fix my toxic overload," I said.

"Wouldn't MDs do that, if it were important?" Logan asked.

"They may not know the toxic connection—or the rebuilding injections that Doctor G's pioneering. It makes sense. As long as I feel the results, let's give it a chance."

"Fair enough," Logan said.

"See you in two days," Jade said.

The thought of making that trip gave me chills. I added hot water to my *waterbed* with my agile toes—another new talent. I settled into weightless sleep, until the water got cold.

15. EMPTY NEST—EMPTY NEST EGG

I spent the next year after my injury in my nest *being still*. To take pressure off my neck, I kept floating in water—known as a symbol of our unconscious in many circles of thought. To soothe my unconscious, Nonnie gave me something to think about during each float:

> *My future is full of hope. My past cannot hold me.*
> *Now and in each moment, all is well and as it should be.*

Although I wanted all of that to be true, when I floated with those thoughts my tears often trickled into my bathwater—as if I didn't believe any of it on an unknown level.

After the first month of floating, there were fewer tears and much less pain. Gradually, I moved beyond thought into a peaceful place when I floated. That shift was slow but steady, the way stone is softened by a stream.

During my first year of recovery, when I wasn't floating in Epsom salt-EDTA baths each day, I was writing the first draft of my novel at my computer. About the only time I left my nest was for a three-day trip to see Doctor G, every three weeks. Each trip was easier to make than the one before it. That kept me going.

After my 7th round of neck injections, 21 weeks after my injury, I saw crocuses blooming through clumps of snow and I knew how they felt. With gentle persistence, I could prepare a simple meal, and sleep on my right side in bed again. *Bloom for me.*

After my 14th round of injections, my neck pain was a fading memory; however, the cost of treatments weighed me down. My divorce support had dwindled down after both children left home, so I had to tap into my retirement fund to pay for big repair bills for my neck and both homes.

With a second year of neck treatments needed before I could resume all of my normal activities, I figured I'd blow through all of my savings if I didn't cut my living expenses quickly. I had to simplify my life. I was concerned how it would affect my kids.

They were happily immersed in their adventures in learning, when I reluctantly gave them another lesson. Via conference call, I told them, "I'm going to sell our Chicago home so I can afford to live in our Santa Fe home. That was the basis of our divorce deal."

In the silent thud that greeted my news, I said, "How do you feel about it?"

Logan said, "Someone will be lucky to raise kids there."

Jade said, "We could hire our drummer's mom to sell our house."

"So you're not upset?" I asked.

"It's not as bad as when you told us about your neck," Logan said.

"And it won't be real till we pack up our stuff," Jade said.

"You'll have a home with me in Santa Fe," I said.

"Our home is Chicago," Logan snapped. So I knew how he felt.

"Or wherever we go," Jade said. "And we'll visit you." So said another Chicagoan.

My empty-nest-hood grabbed me like a fierce undertow, which would drag them down with me if I resisted. *I've got to go with the flow,* I told myself.

"You've grown up," I said. "All is well, and as it should be."

The next day, I hired the drummer's mother as our broker. She'd never sold a home this expensive, so I figured she'd hustle for this big break. Yet, her market analysis stunned me.

There were 400 homes for sale in my price range within a few miles of mine, she informed me. If I wanted to sell in a year or less, she suggested I price my home at least one hundred thousand below appraised value—a strategy used by most of the quick-selling competition. Otherwise, it could take years to attract a buyer. It was my choice, she concluded.

This was a huge decision, and I had to make it fast. My first impulse was to call Walter for advice. *Whoa. That old habit's hard to break, but now's the time. You know what you need to do, Hadley girl.* I priced my home for quick sale.

The next day from an upstairs window, I watched a workman install a fancy sign in my front yard. I felt like I was losing my footing on a steep slope. In that ungrounded moment, the phone rang. I was hoping for a good word when I heard Walter's voice.

"The kids told me your latest troubles," he said. "You're a talented woman with top credentials. Isn't it time to get a job?"

My defenses rose up. "I've been writing my first book, while I had to *be still.*"

"If that book sells like your album, you're lucky you've got a big house to sell. Or sell both homes, if you're desperate," he said.

My thoughts raced toward attack. Against my better judgment, I let him have it. "You bought a Bentley with the money you stopped paying me last year," I shrieked.

"Your point?" he asked.

"My repair bills have doubled. So did your income, when you ascended to your corporate throne. Do you really think you got there alone?"

"My wife supports my work. You always asked me to work less," he said.

I felt as if he'd grabbed my neck and squeezed. A wave of pain made it hard to speak. "Have you forgotten why?" I asked.

"Doesn't matter now," he said. "Our divorce deal can't be changed. It's time to be responsible for your own life."

"I am. Without your advice," I said.

"Good," he said.

"Good-bye." Although I sighed, a river of relief swept over me. *But why?*

It occurred to me that I needed to make that next big break from Walter, before I could stand on my own two feet. I could always value my contributions to his wellbeing and success, even if he never did. And I could create a whole new story without him—with me ascending to my own corporate throne. *But in the meantime, how do I support myself?*

I hadn't finished a draft of my novel, because I was discovering the ending.

I hadn't recorded my new songs, because of recording costs.

I hadn't had an audition since my injury. But I could change that.

I called my agent, Laura, and said, "I'm ready to earn some money for us."

"No more neck brace?" Laura asked.

"I've got the neck of a giraffe."

She chuckled. "Would you do a commercial for an arthritis pain reliever?"

I groaned. "Whatever happened to my sex-starved feature film role last year?"

"You were too smart for that part. But they want a smart boomer to convince the aging herd to stop arthritis pain with their pill."

"Does it harm the liver?" I asked.

"Don't be difficult. You could earn fifty grand for this national spot."

That would cover another year of neck treatments. "What do I wear?"

I quickly changed into *young grandmother casual*. Then I drove through afternoon rush hour to tape my audition before Laura sent the tape to New York.

When I walked into Laura's office, she shrieked, "Your hair."

"Is my windswept look out of date?"

"It makes Einstein's mane look tame," she said.

I saw the girls in the office nod and snicker at their desks, while I felt my hair and realized what had happened. "I've floated in hundreds of salt baths," I said. "And I rarely looked in the mirror."

"That has to change, if you're serious about working," Laura said.

Her tone said she was ready to cancel my audition. So I spoke up. "I'll slick it down before you shoot me. Then I'll be ready for my close up before call-backs."

Her reluctant nod was all I needed to take action before she changed her mind. After making a damp-hair repair at the sink, I met Laura in the taping room and nailed my audition in one take.

"You're back," she said in a cheery voice.

"I know something about pain relief," I said.

Apparently, the client agreed. Two weeks later, I flew to New York to film that commercial. Thrilled to be back in business, my wild woman was roused from a long sleep during my eastbound flight.

To celebrate another big step forward, I used divorce miles to upgrade my ticket to a first-class seat, so I'd get some writing done, undisturbed. Until my seat-mate showed up. I heard him greet nearby passengers by name before he sat down next to me.

While clicking his seatbelt, he said, "Now I'm really glad I made this flight."

I looked up from my manuscript. A dashing, dark-haired man about my age, wearing a crisp oxford and striped tie, was smiling at me. Drawn to his dimples and dark eyes, I smiled back. "Me, too."

"What are you writing?" he asked.

"A novel with a complimentary album of songs in it."

"About?" he asked.

"About a divorced songwriter who turns heartbreak into harmony as she finds love online."

"Based on your own experience?" he asked.

"Inspired by and changed a little, for thematic purposes," I said.

"Have you written anything else?"

I nodded. "For Chicago television. Is this an interview?"

He grinned. "I'm Ted Henderson. I started a new publishing house after 20 years at a biggie. I'd like to publish your book and date you. Are you open to that?"

I froze, as I looked for words. "Uh. Well. Hmm," I stammered. As we sped up for take-off, my thoughts raced: *Remember the trouble Walter caused when he dated someone he worked with. Same for President Clinton. Except the Clintons remained a power couple who work together. So it might work if I dated my publisher. Assuming he's not married.*

He tapped my right temple and asked, "What's going on in there?"

"Sorry," I said. "It's been impossible to date for over a year."

"We're all busy," he said. "Until you meet someone, who could change your life in a snap."

Feeling off balance, I dug up a question that grounded me. "Should I give you a writing sample?"

He revealed those dimples in a big grin. "If you must."

Sensing his true agenda, I rose above it, "Do you have a card so I could mail it?"

He tapped my manuscript, which lay on my lap. "If you give me your first three chapters, I'll give you instant feedback. An offer I rarely make."

I actually giggled as I said, "Santa Fe WuWu works in Chicago. I need publisher, and voila." I pointed to him.

"So you're not heading to the book convention in New York?" he asked.

"I'm filming a commercial there, for a couple days."

"Are your evenings free?"

When I looked into his serious eyes, I was startled by desire. I froze again. "I don't know yet," I said.

He held out his open palm and gave me a hopeful nod. With a playful sigh, I gave him several chapters, and he dug right in. I pretended to be reading my chapter 12, while I watched his reactions out of the corner of my eye.

Occasionally, he'd nod or grin. Once he muttered, "I'm jealous."

I looked at his page number and guessed he was reading about my *Love Outlaw*.

When breakfast was served, I noticed he barely glanced at his Eggs Florentine while he ate. *He's hooked,* I thought.

Halfway into it, he turned to me. "Are you still in love with your Ex?"

"Former. *Ex* crosses him out like he never existed," I said.

"Does that mean, *Yes?*" he asked.

I shook my head. "I love my new life. If my rebirths continue at this pace, I'll be forever one."

"I'm interested. In you and your book," he said.

I didn't know what to say, but my big grin must've said I was interested.

He said, "I've got dinner plans, so let's talk later. At your hotel, around eleven?"

Like a thoroughbred at the gate, my wild woman was raring to go. But my gut told me, *Whoa*. So I said, "I need my beauty sleep for an early call."

He shifted into a deep voice, "Nothing good happens when you stay home alone."

"That's how I wrote my book," I said.

He patted my hand, and then he started reading the next chapter.

The fluttering in my stomach feels like fear. *Fear of being interested in a man? I hope not. Uh-uh. Something about him had put me on guard. I'm proud I saw it.*

As we landed at LaGuardia, Ted straightened up the pages of my chapters and said, "I want my managing editor to read this. Can I take it with me?"

Once again, my gut said, *Whoa*, so I said, "I'd rather send you a clean copy."

Reaching into his coat pocket for a card, he said, "You're not like most writers."

"Thanks," I said, trading my card for his.

Ted leaned closer and I felt his warm breath on my ear. "I'll call you later, Hadley."

I felt a rush of pleasure I'd feared I'd never feel again. "Later," I said.

My unexpected delight lingered—until I had to tuck it away to get in the right mood for my arthritis shoot. That had its own pleasures, culminating in kudos from the client and my joyful anticipation of residual payments each time the spot aired on TV.

My first business trip since my injury ended with one minor disappointment. I'd stayed up past eleven each night in my hotel, in case Ted called. He never did. *Oh, well. I've only got one word to say about a man who doesn't keep his word. NEXT!*

To ease my disappointment, I took a bubble bath in my hotel tub and found comfort in my song I wrote during my uphill climb toward solitary contentment after divorce, **In Love Again**—

> **Rebirth comes from tears you've cried**
> **Sleeping dreams can be revived**
> **You can become what you might have been**
> **Once you fall in love with yourself again**

Ahhh. I did fall in love with me again—when I saw the miracle of my body making me whole after a broken neck and a broken heart. Yes. I love me and my miracle maker. All is well, and as it should be.

The next week, I accepted a two-week subbing assignment for 90 bucks a day. I figured Walter earned that much in each of our 533,600 minutes a year. *Whoa. Don't let that ruin this. Be grateful to have some money coming in.*

In that frame of mind, I enjoyed our class discussions of THE ODYSSEY and our rehearsals of students' skits for their annual Greek Fest. Plus, I worked on my book during three free periods each day. *All without pain. Amazing.*

The study of THE ODYSSEY inspired my major AHA moment. Looking back several years to when I'd subbed during THE ODYSSEY-Greek Fest prep, I remembered how I'd identified with Penelope, the devoted wife who waited and longed for her husband to return home.

Now I was Odysseus, in the midst of my own Odyssey. I faced all challenges the gods threw at me and made choices that determined my fate. That lesson: Priceless.

During lunch break on my fifth day at school, I received an email from Ted.

"Hey, Hadley. We haven't received your chapters. Please resend. Better yet, bring the rest of it with you and read it to me at my home on the beach."

His blur of boundaries bothered me. I had to ask myself, *What do I want most? A publisher? Or a lover?* No contest. I wrote back:

"So glad you're still interested in my work, Ted. I'll send the chapters. But you'll have to wait for the rest

of it until I finish writing it. Hadley."

"Before we go any further, I'd like to propose a Joint Venture arrangement to see if it interests you. Here are the general terms—You'd invest up to $25,000 in editing, design and printing of your book. I'd also invest in that phase, plus I'd pay for the marketing launch. You'd pay for your own marketing platform thereafter. As J-V partners, we'd split all income 50-50."

My reply consisted of two questions:

"What's a 'marketing platform'? What if I sold my soundtrack separately and made a film from my novel?"

"It's how you connect intimately with people in your blog, ezine, teleseminars, etc. so they want to buy your book and other products. We'd have a 50-50 split of all sales. No exceptions. When can you come to see me in Malibu?"

It felt like a lopsided deal, and I had to trust that. I wasn't ready to split profits from years of my work—at least until I saw how much was left in my nest egg when I finished my book. *Can I keep my options open?*

"Blog, ezine, teleseminars are Greek to me, Ted. How do I learn more? Also, I'd like to do some homework on publishing deals, before I respond to yours. Thanks again for your patience and your interest. Hadley."

The next day, Ted sent this email:

"Do you have an extra hour or two a day to build your marketing platform? If so, sign up for the telephone course described in my attachment, so you can take 100 percent responsibility for sharing your message with the world. If not, your book will be turned into toilet paper after no one reads it. Choose wisely. Good luck. Ted."

I knew I could've handled things differently if I'd wanted to pursue the deal or the dance. But neither felt right.

I'd have to say it was easy to let go of a questionable deal from the first publisher I met. But after meeting over a hundred single men, I knew that our instant spark of chemistry was a rare find. I'd stopped wondering if I'd find it again while my thoughts shifted away from my body during my year of floating. *Now I'm back in my body, thanks to Ted.*

Thanks to Ted, the publisher, I signed up for a ten-hour per week marketing course by phone, which would end about the same time as I finished writing my book.

Thanks to Ted, the man who woke my wild woman, I revived my dating profile and uploaded my new headshot, already a year old. Then I re-thought what I sought in a *Mountain Man* before I added my new headline:

> **Kind-hearted SONGBIRD seeking intimate nights
> and enchanting days with a loving, loyal Knight.
> Could that be you?**

16. HELLO FROM SOUTH AMERICA

Hello from South America.

That intriguing greeting caught my eye among several inquiries on my first day back in the SOULFULDATING world. I eagerly opened this note first:

Hello, SONGBIRD

I enjoy enchanting days on my ranch in the Andes Mountains, in a valley of tranquility, where it's springtime year round and many people live past 100.

I'm also seeking intimate nights with a woman like you. I've never been so taken by a photo or a profile. Forgive me, but I had to tell you. I hope you like mine, too.

I'm an American, an author, a former pro-athlete and an architect. I'm designing a peaceful residential community within two thousand acres of natural beauty. It is attracting kind, progressive people from all over the world.

While reading your profile, I was drawn to your kindness, your beauty and your adventurous spirit. When you wrote that you'd traveled to another continent to meet a match, you gave me hope that you'd come to meet me here someday.

I'd like to talk to you. We don't have video-streaming bandwidth available here, but I could drive into town for a clear phone connection. Until then, I will imagine the sound of your voice, and the vision of you enjoying enchanting days and intimate nights with me—
AVERYPRIVATEPARADISE

He sent two recent photos of him in gym shorts, shirtless, while playing volleyball with South American workmen on his ranch. His lean intensity reaffirmed my gut instinct: *He had me at Mountains.*

I wrote back, inviting him to call me the next day at noon. When he did, I was soothed by his voice and by what he chose to tell me during our 1st phone chat:

He had two pups and ten horses that ran freely on his property.

After caring for his mother before she died two years earlier, he felt free to start his new life anywhere in the world.

A friend had told him about this valley in South America. Forty-eight hours after his arrival, he bought his ranch because it felt right. He was led by instinct and always trusted it—with good results. He was working harder than ever—at an age most retire.

Then he dropped a bombshell.

"I've never had children, but I'd still have a child or two with a young woman."

"Why contact me?" I snapped.

"I watch. I see which way life wants me to go," he said. "I'm drawn to you. Tell me about your life, SONGBIRD."

"I'm Hadley Finch. A proud mother of two talented, loving children— who are newly launched but always in my heart. I've learned from my marital mistakes, so I won't repeat them. I'm the artist of my own life. And I'm drawn to you, too."

"Sounds good," he said. "Could I keep calling you—until you feel okay about making the trip to meet me?"

"Sounds good," I said.

I went to sleep that night feeling encouraged. I woke up with one thought: *He's a pioneer.* That warning whisper guided me to explore the possibility when he called me the next evening.

His greeting was enthusiastic, "Have you thought about us as much as I have?"

I was direct. "I've wondered how many women have visited you at the ranch."

"You'd be the second—a year after the first," he said. "I lead a contemplative life, immersed in work. Yet I follow world news, gathering thoughts for my next book."

A smooth segue into his writing, but I pursued my point. "Do you see local women?"

"I'm careful about that. Maybe too careful," he said. "I recently saw one local woman who'd studied in Italy for a year. Sensuous. Worldly. Knew Italian but her English was poor. Communication would be a barrier, so I passed. Is my sexual history important to you?"

"Love leaves traces," I said.

"No traces. My heart was never in it with her. What about you?"

"Nothing's clicked on all cylinders, since my husband."

"Sorry you feel that way. I thought we were building something solid," he said.

"We haven't met yet."

"No? Haven't we had intimate moments?"

His breathy tone tickled my wild woman. "Long distance," I said. "Up close and personal is how I want to know you." Within his exhale, I heard relief.

"Our feelings are fated before we meet. We have little control over it," he said.

"You think so?"

"Powerful sexual forces drove me to call you, to know you and be known by you. There's no casual sex for me, Hadley. If our bond is true and passionate, I'd stop looking and build a new life with you."

Ahhh. Words of a settler, not a pioneer. "No need to guard our hearts?"

With an Arthurian flourish, he said, "If you seek a Knight without armor, my kiss will lift your veil, milady."

His metaphors were on my wavelength. Merrily, I said, "Soon, milord."

"Shall I book your passage?"

My inner brakes clamped down. "Not yet."

As I pondered my resistance, I realized what I needed to do before I was ready to see him. The next day, I used a reward ticket on Southwest for a quick trip to receive my 18th round of injections from Doctor G.

As I got off the treatment table after the hour-long procedure, Doctor G said, "Your thoughts are still broken around your neck. Time to let go of that injury by thinking, *I am healed. I have a perfectly healthy body. Thank you.*"

I repeated it and smiled. "It feels right."

He patted my back, "New beliefs renew you. Healthy thoughts grow healthy molecules."

I felt uplifted, even after paying $1,500 for injections and my daily supplements.

On my way to the airport, I used a library computer to print my boarding pass and check emails. I was pleased to see one from AVERYPRIVATEPARADISE 'til I read it:

"Haven't heard from you, Hadley. Have you lost interest?"

Whoa. It's only been 48 hours. He might be too needy for me. I replied:

"I've been in SFe, where I rarely use the internet. I'll write tomorrow nite."

Upon my return home, I dove into the flow of writing, and I forgot to email him until the following afternoon. He'd already sent me another email:

"You said you'd write last night but you didn't. I'm very aware of patterns; very selective about qualities I seek in a partner. You don't seem ready for a serious relationship, Hadley."

I could've apologized for my oversight, but this felt more urgent:

"We haven't met yet. I like your voice and what you have to say. We could write and chat everyday, and start

to feel close. But I've found that nothing's real until we look in each other's eyes and see the possibilities."

His e-reply was immediate.

"You may not get that chance. If a woman is interested, she'll write multi-dimensional letters about what she likes or doesn't like. You don't engage. Are you too guarded? Or have you lost interest?"

His cold edge made me shiver, as I considered both options. *Neither fits. The truth? I was too busy to think about him, and unaware of his expectations. Do they align with mine? Or should I write him off?* I found my answer:

"I see you're a man who wants to make a relationship his top priority, and I like that. I also like the way you challenged me to look inside and explain myself. That adds depth to our connection.

"I'm definitely interested in meeting you. Sorry I made you doubt that. Since I haven't been in a relationship for many years, I'm used to focusing on other priorities. That's what happened in Santa Fe. I got my house ready for vacation rentals in months I'm not there. I made sure my health was in great shape, before I fly to see you. I had dinner with friends.

"I worked on my book—six hours a day. I also downloaded two of your books on LULU.COM, so I'll get a sense of your vision as an author before we meet.

"You were among my top priorities, but you couldn't have known that unless I told you. I'll be a better communicator from now on. Maybe in Espanol! I studied it in high school, so we'll see how much I remember when I see you.

"I know what it takes to nurture a relationship, and I'd be willing to make that commitment again someday. But until we meet, we can't know if that's possible for us. That's why I hope we meet soon."

He waited a day to reply, so I suspected something was up in his email:

"I want to be totally honest with you, Hadley. I've been corresponding with a very special woman I stumbled upon on our dating site after you showed no interest. She's a tenured professor who plans to visit me during her next break.

"I'm conflicted, because it would be delightful to meet you. What are your feelings?"

My heart sank, but I downplayed my disappointment in my speedy reply:

"Dear John-Juan, Finding two great women to pursue at once is quite a hot streak, so you should play the lottery. I did *conflicted* once, and that was enough. Good luck with your very special woman."

A minute later, I received his email:

"I didn't like your sarcasm. That's a way to avoid feelings rather than express what's really going on. Your feelings?"

Once again, he made me dig into uncomfortable turf, beyond a glib reply:

"I don't use sarcasm. Since our written words are only 20% of total meaning, the heart and soul are revealed in tone and touch—lost in emails. I view that lost mass of meaning as a blank canvas for a reader to project his own feelings onto it. Was that your sarcasm you painted onto my words? Again, I don't use it. I truly felt you were lucky to meet two amazing women at once. But because you're focused elsewhere, I withdrew from competition. I once tried to win back my husband's affection, but I won't do that for a man I haven't even met. I see how dates are made at the speed of write on this site. You sped by me. I've learned my love lesson without the loving, and I feel cheated. I won't make that mistake the next time a great guy contacts me. Sending joy to you and your very special woman."

A half hour later, my phone rang. The ID said UNKNOWN CALLER, but I recognized the voice of AVERYPRIVATEPARADISE as he greeted me with a question:

"What was your love lesson, Hadley?"

"When you get a glimpse of paradise, go for it before it's lost," I said.

His tone softened. "Things are fragile in the beginning. Silence can crush possibilities."

"I see that now," I said.

"We're all trying to figure this out," he said.

I wondered if he heard my smile as I asked, "Did you drive into town to call me?"

Chuckling, he said, "I did. Because what you wrote was astute. I was impressed by your insights. And wisdom. I regret that we didn't connect this deeply before I met someone else."

"By email. That doesn't count," I said.

"What do we do now?" he asked.

"That depends on your feelings for her."

"Could I ask you a very personal question?"

A delicious yearning warmed my voice, "I'd like that."

"You've seen my photos. You may have a sense of me," he said. "How do you imagine our life here?"

I paused to exhale my defenses and surrender to my senses. "Your mountains look soft, like my Sangres," I said. "Love is soft. So I already feel at home, embraced by the Andes and you. Our nights are intimate. Our days serene—rich in work and relationship. We make friends with locals and new arrivals. Each moment we share weaves us together in joy in AVERYPRIVATEPARADISE."

In a long silence, I felt exhilarated and hoped he did, too. "Are you still there?"

"I'm here," he said. "And I want you here with me."

Bam. Our obstacles vanished like ice in a blow torch. "I'm ready."

"Ahhh," he sighed. I was delighted he spoke my language.

The next day he emailed flight options and offered to pay for my tickets. I didn't want to owe him anything, so I booked my flights that left the U.S. four days later.

When I told my children via conference call about my travel plans to meet another SOULFULDATE, they didn't exactly wish me *bon voyage*.

It was déjà vu when Logan asked, "Does he speak English?"

"He was born and worked in the U.S. until he moved to South America last year," I said. "I've gotten to know him by phone, and by reading two of his books and his website essays about his new community in the Andes Mountains."

"Mountains?" Jade asked.

"He said *Mountains* right after *Hello*," I said.

Jade huffed, "What if he faked his picture, like that other dude?"

"I saw recent photos of him on his ranch. I like his looks and his kindness, the most important thing to me," I said.

"What if you re-hurt your neck in a third world country?" Logan asked.

"I just had another treatment. My neck is stronger every day."

Jade said, "If money's a problem, how can you afford it?"

"I'm using divorce miles, for free flights. And I'll have a free guest casita with a chef on the ranch. John lives there in luxury for a thousand a month."

Logan said, "I can't think of another argument. Can you, Jade?"

I redirected their focus. "Have a little faith in me, guys. Send me positive, supportive thought energy, like I do for each of you." I heard reluctance in their *Okay's*. Nevertheless, I gave them my itinerary and the ranch website, and I said they could reach me by cell or email.

When we hung up, I was amused by their third degree. I never had to interrogate them like that, possibly because I'd kept a guiding eye on them so they never got far off course. It was harder for them to return the favor from afar, but I appreciated their efforts. And I expected smooth sailing for my travels abroad.

On departure day, a surprise April blizzard delayed my flight out of Chicago by three hours. Then I missed my connecting flight in Miami by three minutes. *Those damn travel gods have complicated our meeting. Do I go on or go home?*

To help me decide, I gave John-Juan a test. Standing at the gate where my flight just left without me, I called him with news that my trip from Miami would be delayed one day, due to weather.

I could hear him sulk as he said, "It's a two-hour drive to the airport, and I coordinated your arrival with a Canadian couple who will be checking out a ten-acre quinta on the ranch. This week, I'll sell them on reasons to retire here."

"Retire? I'm starting a new career," I shrieked, loud enough to startle people passing by. I waved my apologies to them as I listened to him:

"It's good you'd have your work," he said. "I've got 140 men working on various construction projects, all needing my direction. So we won't see each other in daylight."

Hmm. That won't get me on the plane. I asked, "What about evenings?"

"If we don't have dinner with potential buyers, we'll eat granola while we watch a movie."

Neither option was appetizing. "I can't eat gluten. And we can't get to know each other while watching a movie."

"That's how I unwind, since I don't drink alcohol. I imagine we'd make love after the movie and get to know each other then," he said.

Eager to have a new adventure instead of writing about old ones, my wild woman wanted to seal that deal. But I sensibly continued my love test. "Do you work weekends?"

"My crews stop work at one on Saturday," he said. "The rest of the weekend, I work on my designs for new homes and other structures we're building. I also show the property to locals who drop by. I don't foresee a whole day off, until this project is complete. Don't you work on your book seven days a week?"

"I do, but I'm almost finished with it."

"What's next?" he asked.

"A radio show and a blog with tips to create happy relationships."

"Could you record from here, assuming things worked out with us?"

Although I resisted planning my future on the phone with a stranger, I wasn't ready to disconnect. "I can transmit my reports wherever I am. But none of that matters until we meet."

"You can take a taxi to my place from the airport for 25 bucks. Fate will take it from there. I know you'll spice up my nights, especially if that's our only contact."

Hmm. I'm a spice fan. But why travel so far to repeat the same recipe I followed with my other Type-A man? As I was deciding to return home, a moist, flushed sensation persuaded me to reconsider. *Do I go after a new pleasure that comes with an old lesson? Or do I seek a new one?* My final choice was effortless, so I trusted it.

"You seem too busy for me, John. If that changes, you know how to find me."

"Wasn't your husband a busy man?"

"Still is. He's a corporate White Knight who worked day and night. I wanted more time with his flip side—the Intimate Knight. That's still my ideal."

"You'd toss me back?"

I don't hear enough disappointment. "You'll be snapped up, right after we hang up."

"It's your loss, Hadley."

"Maybe, so. But if it's meant to be, it will be. Somehow. Someday."

"We'll see how it wants to go," he said.

At the rebooking counter, I cancelled my flights to see John-Juan and felt my relief mount up like snow in our April blizzard. No flights were landing in Chicago that day, and there was no reason for me to return to my empty nest anyway.

Turning inside for a clue to my puzzled state, I noticed another yearning that easily could be satisfied. That's when I booked a flight that took me to my tribe.

17. HADLEY'S CROSSING

While I waited with Group 5 to board our flight from Miami to Albu-querque, I second-guessed my decision and wanted a second opinion. Stepping out of line as Groups 1-2 were boarding, I gathered my tribe via conference call and gave them highlights of the adventure I'd just passed up.

Sharon Milton must've tapped into my doubts. "Big mistake, Hadley. Let's face facts. How much longer will men want to be with women our age?"

I tried to sound convincing, "As long as you do what you love and love what you do, you'll attract love—that's the real you."

With startling intensity, Sharon said, "Lyrics from la-la-land. Call John-Juan and get your butt down to South America. You're both writers. You're hot for each other. You're a fool to give up this chance for romance."

Nonnie said, "He's the fool if he's too busy to behold you."

Her daughter, Karly, said, "There's plenty of busy guys in this hemisphere."

"Busy, schmizzy," our friend Max said from her noisy news desk. "He's a good guy who's sexually starved in solitary confinement. An irresistible combination."

Karly groaned, "If you believe his story."

"If you pass, I'll take him," Sharon said. "Nothing's keeping me here, except my friends. My work. My kids' visits during college breaks. Actually, I like my new life, so it would just be a hot affair if I flew down there."

Max spoke up, so I didn't have to. "Go find your own *Mountain Man*. There are a billion out there. We don't have to share."

I gave Sharon another dose of reality. "He's got another woman on standby. She'll probably be on the next plane, if I don't go to him."

"What did you learn when you got slammed during your last trip to meet a man?" Nonnie asked.

"A few things," I said. "What were you thinking?"

"Globetrotting for a date may not be good for you right now," Nonnie said.

"Good point," Max said.

"Do we all agree?" Karly asked.

Finally, Sharon gave us her vote. "Let him come to you. If not, it's Next."

Their supportive sighs sealed my decision, which I announced just as the final passenger entered our boarding tunnel. "What I need most is Tribe Time."

Nonnie said, "We're here, Your Sageness."

Ahhh. I like the sound of that, I thought as I hurried to give the attendant my boarding pass before she closed the gate.

"If the snow stops, I'll see you Friday," Max said.

"Count me in," Sharon said.

With a brisk gait, I boarded my flight and ended our conference call. "Your bunks will be ready for you."

My excitement over mobilizing our tribe was short lived. I spent my first day in seclusion, letting scattered emotions rock me like a rowboat on a stormy sea. Doubtful. Disappointed. Discouraged. Longing. Lonely. A lonely ache gripped me. *Aren't I beyond that? Or am I back where I started when Walter left me? Is that my fate?*

I didn't judge my feelings. I floated with them in my hot bath. Gradually, my sea of pain grew serene and calm. That sweet calm didn't last long either. While I was writing the next day, I received unexpected news on my cell phone.

"Hello, Hadley," John-Juan said. "It's so unlike me...I'm at O'Hare. Can you pick me up?"

My ecstatic, "Yippie," made him chuckle. "So I did the right thing?" he asked.

"At the wrong airport, but your timing's perfect," I squealed.

I knew there was some risk in the solution I proposed to this little predicament. Nevertheless, I placed my trust in my tribe and suggested

John-Juan take the afternoon flight to Albuquerque with Max and Sharon. At five, I picked them up at the airport.

Standing beside my Ford Explorer outside the baggage claim area, I saw John-Juan approach me with one carry-on bag in tow. When our eyes met, he smiled. My heart leapt. *Happy, honorable, handsome.* That's what I thought of him at first glance. As he hugged me, his dark, curly hair smelled pure, like baby shampoo.

Tucked in his arms, I looked up and saw deep creases in his forehead— a sign of our big age difference. *Hmm. I'm okay with that.* "You look like your picture," I said. Then I saw his pensive eyes studying me, while he stroked my cheek.

"So do you, Hadley. Are you a handful, like your friends?"

"In a good way," I said.

As Max and Sharon walked up to us, John-Juan took their bags and tossed them in the back of my Explorer. I accepted their happy hugs.

"There's something about him," Max whispered. Sharon nodded her giddy agreement, so I figured it was something good.

During our 60-mile drive home, John-Juan watched my profile behind the wheel more often than the passing scenery. *Sit up straight,* I often reminded myself. Sharon and Max napped in the back seat, giving us privacy to get acquainted.

"It was courageous of you to let me come here," he said.

"And of you, for coming."

"After the Canadian couple was snowed in, I wondered what was stopping me, besides fear. And that's not real," he said.

I gently disagreed. "Fear had choked the blood supply to my heart— until I stopped fighting my breakup and started to see how all was well and as it should be in each moment. To get there, I needed help from my friends." Gesturing to the back seat, I added, "My Tribe of Blondes."

Glancing at the dark-haired sleeping beauties, he looked perplexed. So I gave him the simple explanation. "Not a hair color, it's a joyful, enthusiastic spirit that we're born with. The secret is to keep that spirit alive to be an active member of the Tribe."

His fingers clicked a nervous code on the armrest. "I'll keep an open mind."

In a lull, he reached for his phone and checked messages. In the third one, I overheard a woman's voice ask if she could stay with him this week, while her house was being painted. That tugged at my Achilles Heel, so I watched each nuance of his reaction.

He turned to me and said, "You saved me from an uncomfortable situation."

"With a woman you've dated?" I asked.

He shook his head. "Janet is bi-polar. She often stops by without an invitation."

"And you invite her in?" I asked.

"I want to help her," he said. "She's 47, never married due to her health. She left all her things behind in the U.S. to start fresh. I know how that feels."

"To shed your old skin and grow new?" I asked.

"A path to clarity," he said. "That's what I'm hoping for this weekend."

When he smiled, I felt a surge of something far more primal.

"I've got a question for you," he said. "Is civilization doomed to continue its downward spiral? Or can each individual's actions to improve the health of our planet reverse the trend?"

Whoa. What a mood changer. If that's his love test, I'm glad I did my homework. "That's a theme in two of your books."

He smiled, as if I passed. "What's your take on it?" he asked.

Slowing down to take the bypass off I-25, I said, "Are you a spiritual man?"

He shrugged. "I don't know what spiritual means."

"Spirit means *breath* in Greek. I see spirituality as the breath of love. The force that moves mountains is in each of us. Imagine if we combined our efforts," I said. My first attempt to match the musings in his books earned this response: a big, loud yawn.

"Sorry," he sighed. "I haven't slept well. Stressed by our meeting."

"No pressure. We're just getting to know each other, which won't be easy with a house full of friends. You can retreat to your guest house, whenever."

As he thanked me, I felt Sharon's shoe pushing my seatback—a sign she was eavesdropping and she might not approve of his separate quarters. *Oh well. She can't change my mind about my escape hatch. What if I don't want to use it?*

"You're smiling," he said.

"How does it feel to be with a younger babe?" I asked.

"You looked younger in your photos. And lighter, like a waif."

I was hurt by his disappointed tone. "They're a year old. A tough year."

"You look older. Stronger."

He poked a sore spot, so I shrieked, "What kind of idiot says that out loud? I left the last guy over that."

"Sorry, but I need a certain aesthetic," he said.

"You're entitled," I said, calming down. "When you close your eyes, how do you see me?"

"Not a guy thing," he said.

"It's a heart thing. Got one?" He silently watched the scenery for the rest of our ride.

When we parked on my gravel drive, John-Juan jumped out of my Explorer and pulled all of their bags out of the back gate. In our private moment inside, Max poked me and whispered, "If he doesn't think you're fabulous, screw him."

"Don't screw him," Sharon said. "He's got a jerky side."

"He's being honest," I said, noticing my urge to give him a break.

"Hurtful," Max said.

"If I don't like how I feel around him, he won't be around long," I said.

As we stepped outside, my mountains were divinely painted in a glorious sheen at sunset. Pointing toward them, I said, "See our purple mountain majesty?" Gazing at our big sky, Max and Sharon rang out a chorus of *Wow*'s.

John-Juan clasped my index finger in his hands and pressed it against his chest. "Did you know the Incas never pointed at their mountains?" he said. "They believed mountains were closer to God and deserved respect. They gave them names of honor, so they could refer to them without pointing."

That didn't feel like a reprimand, so I said, "I like learning from you."

"Main reason to date a much-older man," Sharon said in a snide tone.

"We're not dating," I said.

He squeezed my hand, "Not yet." I returned the squeeze.

As we walked through the wooden gate into the cozy courtyard of my adobe hacienda, I assigned Max and Sharon to Logan and Jade's bedrooms in the main house.

Then I led John-Juan into the guest casita. He looked up at the tree trunks (vigas) lining the 16-foot ceiling and glanced around the *great room*. "Great wood. Great furniture. Great feel."

"My first design," I said, proudly. "The only change I had to make was to vent the drier in the kitchen on an outside wall."

He turned to a painting and stepped closer, looking for the artist's signature. "A Gauguin?" he asked.

Proudly, I said, "I copied his *Day of the gods* at the Art Institute Chicago. Why not learn from the masters?"

His faced looked flushed. "I'm way out of my comfort zone," he said.

Without thinking, I touched his hand, "How can I help?"

His eyes brightened. "You just did."

Crossing my courtyard, I noticed how it was changing its palette from dormant tan to vibrant green. I took that cue from mother nature.

In my bedroom, I changed from *chauffeur casual* into an off-the-shoulder knit dress. Glancing in my magnifying mirror, I noticed my skin was looking desert dry and thinner than normal. *Are good oils flushed out with bad toxins? Ask Doctor G how to replenish them.*

While I massaged body butter into my arms, calves, thighs, I imagined John-Juan's hands lathering moisture into my parched skin—*like water in a drought.*

When I walked out of my room, he was standing at my door. "You have a glow."

I whispered, "You've eased into my fantasies."

He raised his eyebrows and took my hand. I led him into the kitchen and proudly introduced him: To Doctor G and his girlfriend, Lauren, who were assembling a tray of endive and pate with raw-Morbier. To Nonnie, who was trimming stems of yellow roses and arranging them in a vase. To Karly, who was stirring the pot of hunter's stew I'd prepared before I left for the airport.

After a hearty greeting, Karly said, "Billy's coming for dinner. He wants to come home."

"What do you want?" I asked.

"To get good at forgiveness," Karly said.

"I wish I'd been a quick study," I said.

Nonnie said, "So you didn't take Walter back when he came to his senses. He moved on with someone wonderful like you. When will you let someone into your life?"

I felt she'd turned on me with her unflattering portrait. "When it's right," I snapped.

In a supportive tone, John-Juan said, "Why dive into a rocky sea?"

"Exactly," I said.

"Two cautious souls," Nonnie observed, without a hint of criticism. Yet I felt it was unfair.

"Caution didn't get him on the plane," I said.

He nodded. "Although I am careful," he said. "Again and again, I've seen how break-ups bring out the worst in women. I don't have time for that nonsense."

"That nonsense caused my greatest growth," I said. "Not that I want to go back there. I'd prefer to learn from joy."

"Wouldn't that be nice," he said. I noticed an optimistic twinkle in his eyes.

"Hey, everybody," Sharon and Max cheered as they joined the party. Dressed in Southwestern skirts and cowgirl boots, they gave out winsome hugs on their way to the bar. Doctor G helped them pour Le Clique that he brought with his appetizers.

When Billy arrived, I saw some grey hair and a spare tire he didn't have when he left Karly. With his beaming smile, he seemed genuinely delighted to see us again.

Doctor G gave Billy a flute of champagne; then he held up his own for a toast: "I'd like to thank Hadley for reuniting our dear friends tonight, and I'd like to welcome her new friend, John. Don't be fooled by her kindness. Hadley got back on her feet with more inner strength than anyone I know. To Hadley."

John-Juan tossed me a puzzled look. *Damn. Doctor G shouldn't blab my old health issues. Oh well.* I clicked a circle of flutes and sealed his lovely toast.

Doctor G continued, "Now let's drink to a woman who'll need great strength to be married to me. To my favorite, future bride, Lauren. I've got it right this time."

Everyone applauded, as our impromptu reunion became an engagement party. John-Juan whispered to me, "He got it right, after how many tries?"

"I'm not sure," I said, enjoying a whiff of his aftershave. "They've dated long enough to know each other's quirks. He loves her kids. Marriage makes sense."

Holding his chin like Rodin's *Thinker*, he said, "Most mid-life couples moving to the ranch are together because they want to be. They see no need for a legal contract. Your feelings?"

I shrugged. "That simplifies finances, unless you reach the common-law mark."

"Money's your top concern?" he asked in a disappointed tone.

Why should I let him burst my bubbly mood, after my first bubbly in over a year? "Nope," I said. "What do you do for fun, John-Juan?"

He furrowed his brow. "I'm not a Lothario."

Skeptical, I said, "*Again and again* you've had breakup nonsense."

"A cycle I'd like to break. I used to desire desire, and chase it like a dumb ass."

I liked the feel of his unvarnished portrait, so I added to mine. "I wouldn't take my husband back, because I wanted to go have some fun like he did. Never had so much fun since I broke up our family." My energy tanked, and I looked away.

While giving me a comforting pat, he said, "Can you drop your whip?"

Whoa. Do I beat myself up? I was startled by Sharon's high-pitched voice:

"Yeah. Who hasn't had a pioneer phase," she said, as if brushing off lint from a vinyl record. Apparently, she'd been watching us paint our self-portraits, unnoticed.

"I go for inspiration, not punishment," I said.

"Your unconscious urges are a million times stronger," he said.

"Do you know how to deactivate them?" I asked.

"Only through my reading, but I'm intrigued," he said.

Wow. He's on my wavelength, I thought as Sharon stepped between us. "I'll help with dinner, if we eat sooner," Sharon said.

I gave her the tools to mix the avocado dressing on the salad, and she dug in. Then I offered John the soup ladle. "Would you dish out the hunter stew?"

Lifting the lid, he stirred the steaming broth and scrunched up his face.

"What's wrong?" I asked.

Shaking his head, he said, "It might upset you."

"I let things roll off my back. Shoot."

He pursed his lips, as if considering a weighty matter. "Did you know eating meat causes more global warming than driving a car?"

"Another vegetarian," Sharon sighed.

He raised his eyebrows defensively. "I eat fish occasionally."

While trading John's ladle for Sharon's tongs, I said, "I drive a hybrid at home, so that makes up for eating grass-fed meat, which keeps me alkaline. Beef *beefed me up* when I lost 20 pounds during my breakup."

"Is that how you got back on your feet?" he asked.

Clearly, that toast was still on his mind, so I gave him some clarity.

"I'm one of those ducks in a shooting gallery. When I get shot down I bounce back up."

Max spoke up behind me. "She's not inviting you to take aim."

"True," I said, realizing John and I would have no private chats during the party. I also knew it was *Now or NEXT* in terms of getting to know each other. I said, "I'd like to drop my armor."

"For armour?" he asked tenderly.

When he smiled, I felt a delicious shift in our chemistry. So did our audience. Max uttered an earthy, "Hhm-Hhmmmm."

Sharon pointed to John and me. "You'd be one of those couples who look alike. Not hair color. Same bone structure."

Washing his hands at the sink, John smiled, "You think our DNA's compatible?"

Sharon answered first, "Who cares? You're way past the baby stage."

"I'm not ruling anything out," he said, holding up his wet hands expectantly. I gave him a clean towel. "Would you ever adopt a baby? I mean, what will you do with the next 30-40 years of your life, Hadley?"

Max and Sharon rolled their eyes. I was flattered by his question, but my intentions never wavered. "If you want a baby, I want that for you. But not for me."

"Even if you had help during the day?" he asked. He clearly had no idea what it took to raise a child.

"I've earned some time for me," I said, chuckling at the memory of occasional frustration with demands of parenting that I'd vented in **A Woman's B.S.—**

> *Oh why did we get a B.S degree*
> *When all we see is a sports utility*
> *We're burning up gas. Going nowhere*
> *Wasting our brains. The kids don't care*

Of course I knew my kids cared I was there to launch them, and I was glad I did so. But do I want to repeat the process at this late date? I asked myself. "A baby's a deal breaker," I said. "So stop the interview and have some fun."

"Just hang out?" he asked awkwardly, as if trying on an ill-fitting suit. Then he grabbed a knife and chopped a mound of fresh herbs for the salad with a surgical precision that tickled me.

Outside his gaze, Sharon's wave dismissed him. I understood her reasoning. Yet I thought his intense focus on task could be gratifying in the bedroom. *Whoa wild woman.*

We dined at my oversized round table where John sat between Max and Sharon, across from me and Nonnie. At my left, Billy and Karly touched and talked tenderly to each other. So did Doctor G and Lauren. When John caught my eye, I felt a rush of heat from my groin to my chest. *Ahhh. Give some credit to my first Bordeaux in ages.*

While I helped Nonnie dish out her chocolate flan dessert, John showed the gang some photos of his ranch on his laptop. My favorite shot was of the construction team gathering for volleyball after work in John-Juan's yard, for its provocative beauty.

Back at my round table during dessert, I was surprised when John-Juan launched a personal conversation in front of my curious friends. "You've created your own paradise," he said, "where you see the world from a privileged viewpoint."

Gently, I corrected him. "A hopeful view doesn't cost a dime."

He nodded. "Would you ever give all this up and come to me?"

My resistance was mounting but I didn't know which argument to use first. Max beat me to it. "Why not cross that bridge when you get there?"

"I'd like to leave on Sunday with a decision made," he said.

"That can't be rushed," I said. Everyone agreed—except John, who put on an orator voice as if he expected to wow us with his eloquent argument:

"Until you commit, there is hesitancy," he said. "The moment you commit, providence moves too. All sorts of unforeseen events issue from that decision, which we could not dream would come our way. So whatever you can do, or dream, you can begin it. Boldness has genius, power and magic in it. Will you be bold?"

Deflecting the pressure for an answer, I said, "I love that Goethe quote."

"It's used to sell stuff all over the internet," Max said, as if busting him.

Casually, John said, "I read the original in German."

Max studied his face. "I think I believe you."

Ahhh. He's smart and humble. I shared my spin on Goethe. "Out here, providence is known as *mountain gods*. And magical, unforeseen events are *Santa Fe WuWu*."

"You're evasive," John said. "Not ready for a serious relationship."

Billy scratched his new sideburns. "I thought you just met her."

"My first instincts are always right," John said.

Nonnie said, "Hadley's used that argument to run from a hundred first dates."

I shrugged. "True."

Catching my gaze, John said, "I'd like to run toward, not away."

Karly turned to him. "So you're not too busy for a relationship?"

"That's between Hadley and me," he said. Karly stiffened. Easing a tense moment, Doctor G said, "We look out for her like family."

"Well, then, you're all invited to visit the ranch," John said, directing his next words to me. "With your children. I'd want them to be part of our lives for this to work."

"They're young adults," I said. "What if they don't want to go?"

His eyes flickered, as if scanning images on his mind's white board. "I could hire a couple young architects to run things when I go to them."

"That's progress," Nonnie said. Our round table heartily agreed.

"Deal or No Deal?" Max asked, while stacking our dessert plates on hers. "Tune in soon to see what develops between them while we do dishes and finish the red."

As Max herded everyone into the kitchen with dirty dishes in hand, I told John, "Privacy. At last." This time, I couldn't resist a yawn. "It's not you," I sighed. "It's the wine."

Reaching for my hand, he said, "Walk me home?"

We entered my courtyard where I noticed some curious eyes glancing our way from the kitchen window. I led John up the winding staircase to my roof deck, where we gazed at our big sky, displaying billions of diamonds on black velvet.

As his fingertip stroked my cheek, I turned to him expectantly. Then he drew me into his arms for our first kiss. When I closed my eyes, I saw the twinkling light of fireflies and thought, *I could love him.*

With a breathy whisper, he said, "Would you talk dirty?"

I fumbled, "I didn't…I don't…Well, how?"

There was a sexy grin in his voice as he said, "I want to dazzle your fine ass."

"Ooooh." I snuggled up for another kiss. He had a different impulse. Drawing me against his chest, he swayed gently, "It's a whole dance—all spontaneous in a loving relationship."

When I kissed his neck I felt his lifeblood pulsing beneath my lips. "We're warming up to each other," I said.

He smiled. "What if we found that needle in the hay? How do we proceed?"

My wild woman leapt, "Shall we go inside or lie down under the stars?"

"I meant—do I go back and see how we feel when we're apart? Or do I leave here with a plan in place?"

"You're a mood changer," I said.

"Why waste our sexual energy if there's no future in it?"

"Odd for you to say."

"You said you'd go for Paradise before it's lost. Good instincts," he said.

He forced me back into thinking mode, which irritated me. I never meant to start a debate when I told him that the most I'd see him would be a couple months at a time—so I'd be here for my children and their children someday.

"It's an unhealthy place. Don't you want your family to have clean air, water, food?"

"You left the country to get it. I'd rather stay here and fix it."

"It's unfixable—when it's government for corporations, not for people. Our democratic dream is critically wounded."

His bleak view could drag me down. Time to give him my final love test. "Aren't we wired to turn wounds into wise action, personally and politically?"

"You're a dreamer," he said as if a putdown.

"With a brighter view than yours. Is it irreconcilable differences?" I asked.

"It's the kind of discourse I need in a relationship. I also believe in right action," he said, his voice turning playful, "If we helped our neighbors stay healthy, they wouldn't pee prescription drugs into water we drink."

That made me laugh. "You'd fit right in here," I said.

Now grinning, he held my hand and led me to my rooftop chaise. As we nestled in each other's arms, he said, "I'd like one home, not three. A simple life."

"I'd like to love life the way it shows up. And love myself and others, however we show up," I said.

"Including me?" he asked sweetly.

Tenderly, I pointed out a big bump in the road. "If you'd like a baby, a younger woman is your best choice. If you'd like to create the greatest version of you, then I could be your muse. And you'd be mine. We'd still come together to create new life."

"Was that a proposal?" he asked.

What an unfortunate moment for a switch to be flipped off in my brain, totally out of my control. "I can't drink," I sighed. Fade to black.

The sun was tickling my eyes when I woke up in John's cuddly embrace on that cramped chaise. He was still sleeping, so I kept quiet, feeling, *It's great to be alive. Thank you.*

Max clanged the triangle bell in the courtyard and shouted, "Chow time. I hope you guys saved some energy for a hike."

Unfortunately, we did. Another day, another chance for romance, I thought as I stroked his forehead. When he opened his eyes and smiled, I presented our morning plans. He was game. *Another good sign.*

We devoured a *cowboy breakfast* prepared by Max and Sharon. John and I did a quick cleanup. Then we changed into hiking clothes and met the usual suspects at our favorite mountain trail. John kept pace with the chatty pack, while Doctor G slowed down to be with me.

"John's an impressive guy," he said.

I nodded. "But I won't visit him until I've got my health back. Why subject any guy to my slow recovery?"

"How else do you see him deal with real life? That's key at this stage. Have you told him your situation?" Doctor G asked.

"I don't lead with that story. It's not who I am," I said.

As if on cue, John looked back and slowed down until we caught up. "Looks like a serious discussion. Want a second opinion?" he asked lightly.

"With Hadley's permission," Doctor G said.

I shrugged. "I'm the marble and you've got the chisels."

Doctor G said, "You're a canary in a coal mine, who survives a toxic assault and guides the rest of us out of the dark mine."

"Not the life purpose I had in mind," I said.

"Notice how your body protected you from the environmental poisons until your children left home. Then you got the wake-up call," Doctor G said.

"Wake up call?" I asked.

"To reality. We care for our bodies and our environment the same way because we're made of the same stuff. So the whole planet is home and all children are our children. Is it a coincidence you're an empty-nested writer who's experienced this reality in painful yet profound ways? Now you've got the time and talent to do something about it. Exquisite, isn't it?"

"Not that you offer personal advice, Doctor," I teased. Doctor G grinned. John turned to me, "You survived a toxic assault?"

I knew he might move on when he heard my story. If so, I'd rather know it now. So I asked Doctor G to explain my condition and treatment. As he did so, John asked questions and seemed to accept his theories, unlike other men in my life.

Unintentionally, I tuned them out when I saw a cluster of daffodils waving at me in the breeze, reminding me I *did nothing to prevent my mom's death. Damn. I know I can't change it. Yet I can't carry that regret anymore. How do I love the thoughtless me? Nobody's perfect. That's okay with me.*

For the first time since my mom left me, I lifted my dark veil and tossed it behind me. I let myself see the radiance of her smile in the sun, dancing on those yellow blooms. *Ahhh. Clarity.*

I heard John ask me something and I was touched by his tender tone, the way a sweet sonata soothed each cell before my brain recognized what was heard through my ears. "I wasn't listening, sorry."

"Are you strong enough to travel to me? Or should I travel to you?" John said.

I reminded him that I was on my way to see him but something made me turn back. He told me that was workable. *Another good sign.*

As we circled around the winding trail, my heart started racing long before I caught sight of the old obstacle looming ahead: That damn log bridge. When we approached it, Nonnie, Karly, Billy and Max already had crossed. They were talking Sharon across. After she reached the other side, we all cheered.

Standing on our side of the bridge, Lauren opened her arms when she saw Doctor G. After a smooch, they zipped across, as if making a yellow light while it turned red.

John opened his arms for my hug, and I felt his jitters. *Damn. His fear's contagious.* "Let's take a long cut and meet up with them," I said.

He shook his head and gestured toward the log bridge. "You go first."

I wanted to live up to his expectations, but I shrieked, "I've never made it across."

"I've got your back. You're already there," John said.

I wanted to believe him. Slowly, I turned toward a chorus of encouraging shouts. Taking baby steps onto the log, my right foot slid on traces of spring snow. I looked down and froze, watching clumps of snow rafting on whitewater far below my boots.

I heard Nonnie yell, "BREATHE". So I took a balancing breath.

Karly shouted, "Look at me." I did. Like a magnet, I was drawn to her smile. But I still couldn't move my feet. In my frozen state, I looked inside and assessed what was holding me back. *Expectations of doing things right? Fears of making mistakes? How do I love the scared, imperfect me?*

I took a deep breath and took her with me. From the bottom of my diaphragm, I shrieked like a banshee launching an attack. That force propelled me across the log like rocket fuel.

Savoring cheers and hugs from my tribe, it felt like I crossed from *Whoa* to *Wow*, and I wished my children had been there to see it. *Whoops. I forgot about John.* When I turned around, he looked like a petrified statue, stuck in the middle of the log.

I shouted, "Look at me, John-Juan." He did. Then his gaze never strayed. As the tribe got behind his crossing with shouts of support, each deliberate step led him into my arms. His heart was pounding as I hugged him. Everyone applauded his feat, and then we continued around the spiral path.

Lagging behind with me, John put his arm through the crook in mine. "You got me unstuck," he said.

I beamed, "A big day for both of us."

"Know how?" he asked. Before I could imagine it, he said, "I saw you naked. And I couldn't wait to make love with you. As John-Juan—but only for you."

BAM. I saw that happening right there on the carpet of red earth. I felt flushed when I turned to him. "Are you the same man I met yesterday?"

He chuckled. "You have a special affect on me." Gripping my belly like a melon, he said, "We'll get this toned, when you spend time with me."

Hmm. That feels more like a healthy nudge than a criticism. I slid my hand over his and felt the heat of his palm patching a pinhole in my soul. Breathlessly, I asked, "Know what's happening?"

"Something we can't ignore," he said.

With a firm hand against the curve of my back, he drew me closer to his lips. Then he balked. "There's one more thing to clear up," he said. "What if we don't make it?"

Hmm. I can be a mood changer, too. "I'd burn your clothes in a bonfire. Then I'd stalk you and your next lover." His worried gaze made me grin. "Or there's Plan B: I'd let you go with my love lessons learned. Then I'd say, *Next.*"

With a hopeful lilt in his voice, he asked, "And if we *do* make it?"

Stroking his chapped lips, I said, "I'd banish *Next* and savor *Now*, where all is well and as it should be. Isn't that where we live happily ever after, no matter what happens?"

He creased his brow, "So I've heard, but I can't get my mind behind it."

During my year of *being still*, I'd learned how to float beyond that stream of thinking that can lead to paralysis. *Does he need a little nudge?* "You're not that voice in your head. Sshhh," I whispered.

His whole face softened and then he spoke to me without words. His kiss was a taste of paradise that ended my search for a *Mountain Man*. For *Now*—and quite possibly until we rode off into whatever great adventure comes next. *Ahhh.*

> **Hearts are meant to soften**
> **Admit your fears, find your grace**
> **It takes strength to show your weakness**
> **So let's burn in the *Fire Of Love***
> **Let's burn in the *Fire Of Love* —- *Fire Of Love***

A GIFT FOR YOU

I'd like to thank you for buying my debut novel by giving you a gift of 14 songs inspired by my real-life journey from lost love to the Fire Of Love. As you read the novel, you will see what inspired the lyrics for each song. That's why I'd like to give you a chance to download them for free.

Talented singers, musicians and composers from Santa Fe, New Mexico brought my song lyrics to life. Several songs have received AA radio airplay from Maine to Maui. These songs share secrets for surviving a break up, reviving your dreams and falling In Love Again. I hope you enjoy them.

You may **claim your FREE bonus** music when you visit:

www.TribeOfBlondes.com/bonusmusic

Simply type in your first name and your primary email address. Then you gain instant access to all 14 songs!

Thanks again for reading this novel. If you'd like to stay in touch with the *Tribe Of Blondes*, I invite you to do so in several ways:

A Special Invitation To Our Readers

The *Tribe Of Blondes* hosts telephone interviews with relationship experts who share secrets for creating happy relationships. These telephone gatherings are affectionately known as TelePowWows in the *Tribe Of Blondes*. Would you like to listen in or ask questions during these calls?

I will give you the call-in details for each interview, when you sign our guest list at:

www.TribeOfBlondes.com/relationshipsecretsguestlist

An Invitation For Our Single Readers

The *Tribe Of Blondes* is developing a video interactive membership site to safely introduce soulful singles for social networking, travel adventures and cultural-edutainment activities. Would you like to help me develop our new site for singles?

I'd like to hear your ideas about what activities and benefits you'd like to see in our membership site. You will get a one-month free trial membership as my thanks for telling me your ideas, comments or questions when you visit:

www.TribeOfBlondes.com/tribeofsingles

Interested In Our Online Novel?

Our readers will receive a huge discount when you buy the online version of *Tribe Of Blondes*. It is the first multimedia novel with songs, videos, the art mentioned in this novel—plus an audio-book of my reading the unabridged novel to you. Sold separately the online novel, album and audio-book cost $70. You may buy the online package for just $7, when you visit:

www.TribeOfBlondes.com/onlinenoveldiscount

Thanks again for your interest in the *Tribe of Blondes*. I'm excited for you to share our adventures!

Hadley Finch